Cry Havoc

by Allan R. Kenward

SAMUEL FRENCH, INC.
45 West 25th Street NEW YORK 10010
7623 Sunset Boulevard HOLLYWOOD 90046
LONDON TORONTO

ISBN 0 573 63003 8 Printed in U.S.A. #5184

Copy of program of the first performance of CRY HAVOC as produced at the Morosco Theatre, New York.

LEE SHUBERT

PRESENTS

CRY HAVOC

BY

ALLAN R. KENWARD

STAGED BY MR. KENWARD

SETTING BY ALBERT JOHNSON   LIGHTING BY MOE HACK

CAST

(As they speak.)

DOC . . . . *Ann Shoemaker*
SMITTY . . . . *Katherine Emery*
FLO . . . . *Florence Rice*
PAT . . . . *Thelma Schnee*
CONNIE . . . . *Katherine Locke*
STEVE . . . . *Carol Channing*
SUE . . . . *Margaret Phillips*
ANDRA . . . . *Helen Trenholme*
NYDIA . . . . *Florence MacMichael*
HELEN . . . . *Julie Stevens*
GRACE . . . . *Muriel Hutchison*
SADIE . . . . *Ruth Conley*
NATIVE WOMAN . . . . *Teresa Teves*

SCENE

A converted gun emplacement adjacent to Bataan Peninsula, early in 1942.

"First in Spite of Hell"
Motto of the defenders of Bataan.

ACT I

SCENE 1. Afternoon.
SCENE 2. Four days later—11:30 P. M.

ACT II

Late afternoon, several days later.

ACT III

SCENE 1. Shortly before dawn, the following morning.
SCENE 2. Several hours later.

STORY OF THE PLAY

The play has been hailed as a female "Journey's End" and tells the story of some nurses on Bataan. The cast is composed entirely of women; we see the characters in a sort of dugout, subjected to gunfire, and we watch the individual characters emerge in a sort of collective reaction to war.

There is the strong-minded doctor, efficient and untroubled. There is her assistant, restrained and poised, and there are the volunteer nurses—a vacuous Southern girl, who might as well be in the Civil War; a swaggering bully; a couple of timid aesthetes who believe the war is a religious war; an ex-burlesque girl; a big, strapping gal from a lumber camp, with an honest confusion regarding herself; and the inevitable spy.

They get on one another's nerves, arrest the wrong person as a spy helping the Japs, and finally confront the real traitor. At the end they find that they are rescued from their buried dugout only to face the firing squad.

DESCRIPTION OF CHARACTERS

DOC MARSH is an elderly woman of great activity.

SMITTY is a handsome girl in her early thirties. Lean, competent, thorough and cool.

FLO HARRIS is a big girl—the kind we see grinning at us from news-reels as the winner of a corn-husking contest. Slow of speech and action, she is a bit of a philosopher in her own way.

PAT CONLIN, a fiery little pug-nosed girl with a good consignment of freckles, who has a bit of a swagger about everything she does.

GRACE LAMBERT, a well-formed and attractive girl of medium height.

HELEN DOMERET, a lovely statuesque blonde, who carries herself like a model and whose thoughts continually run to men.

NYDIA JOYCE, a cute little literal-minded Southerner.

SUSAN and ANDRA WEST, auburn-haired English girls. Susan, the elder, is the leader, continually protecting and looking out for the more fragile Andra.

CONSTANCE MARKS, a Dresden-doll of a girl, beautifully turned out, delicate and, one might think, too fragile for the work ahead.

STEPHANY FOLDEN (STEVE), a large, raw-boned, muscular gal who carries herself like a man.

SADIE, a substantial middle-aged woman.

ACT ONE

SCENE I

The interior of a bomb-proof shelter near Bataan (originally the concrete foundation for one of Bataan Peninsula's big coast artillery guns now converted into sleeping quarters for its defenders). The furnishings are "catch as catch can." With the exception of a hospital medicine chest and the two decker iron bunks which line the walls, all are products of native craftmanship. The shelter, or "dug-out," is entered from the road above by means of a flight of stairs which are visible when the door rear Center is open. A door down Left leads into a corridor which services a store room, lavatory and small field kitchen. The door up Right leads into another passageway and thence to a small mobile hospital. There is a table Left Center surrounded by several boxes and stools. A desk above Left door is served by a dilapidated chair. A wash basin in the corner up Left has found its way into the shelter from some ship's fittings. The walls are covered with pictures of women cut from magazines and newspapers, mementos of the recent occupancy of a number of officers who have since been moved to Corregidor. Over the door Center is scrawled in charcoal the motto of Bataan, "First In Spite Of Hell." A small acetylene lamp hangs Center and supplies the main source of light.
AT CURTAIN: *The door Center opens and an elderly woman of great activity enters. She is* DOC MARSH.

She takes off her helmet and draws her sleeve across a wet forehead and grey hair. She drops the helmet on the desk and beats some of the dust from her work-stained drab uniform as she quickly surveys the room.

DOC. [*Calling off Right.*] Smitty. [*Crosses to door down Left.*] Smitty—you in there?

SMITTY. [*From Right.*] Coming. [*Enters.*] Almost ready for customers inside. [SMITTY *is a handsome girl in her early thirties. Lean, competent, thorough and cool. She looks tired and is.*]

DOC. Anybody helping you?

SMITTY. Lieutenant Holt brought over a couple of native stretcher bearers.

DOC [*Watching for* SMITTY'S *reaction.*] Don't imagine he was much help—

SMITTY. [*Significantly.*] No. Say, what's this burst of activity up here for? We've more work at the hospital than we can handle.

[*They join in checking the bunks and tossing blankets on each.*]

DOC. General MacArthur's moving his whole force up on the Bataan Peninsula. They're setting up a mobile unit here to complement the staff at the hospital.

SMITTY. With what?

DOC. A number of those girls who were evacuated to Cab Cabin have volunteered. Some of them will be quartered here.

SMITTY. [*Bitterly.*] Nurses, or some more of those wet-nosed kids with ten thumbs.

DOC. [*Amused.*] Why, Smitty, I believe you sound bitter.

SMITTY. Why not? By the time they know enough to duck, there'll be about two of them left.

DOC. [*More business-like.*] They've all had some training at the base hospital—

SMITTY. [*Disgusted.*] Some training.

DOC. You'll make up the difference.

SMITTY. Me?

DOC. I'm counting on you to help them fit in.

SMITTY. I sure must be slipping when you pick me for a wet-nurse.

DOC. You need the rest, Smitty. You're the best girl I've got and I'd lose you if you were to keep going at the rate you have—purely selfish on my part.

SMITTY. I'll be damned if you couldn't sell a set of false teeth to Hirohito—and make him wear them.

DOC. Flo Harris will come over to lend a hand, and I'm having the nurses' cook from the base hospital stationed here to handle the meals.

SMITTY. Guess I should be thankful, though, it's the safest shelter in the sector.

DOC. How do you know?

SMITTY. It was the officers' quarters—wasn't it? [*Off stage we can hear someone whistling. The Center door opens and* FLO HARRIS *enters. She is a big girl—the kind we see grinning at us from news-reels as the win-*

ner of a corn-husking contest. Slow of speech and action, she is a bit of a philosopher in her own way. Her uniform, like the DOC's *and* SMITTY's *bears the signs of hard wear.*] Greetings, Flo.

FLO. Hi, Smitty—Doc—

DOC. Hello, Flo.

FLO. This our new diggin's?

DOC. Right. I want you to help Smitty break in some volunteers who were just sent down.

FLO. I suppose they're the bunch of lambs Major Williams has lined up in front of the hospital—tellin' them the facts of life.

SMITTY. Or vice-versa.

DOC. He'll keep half of them there for the hospital and send the rest of them over here. [*Starts out Left.*] Let me know when they arrive.

SMITTY. Yep.

DOC. By the way—they haven't sent us any information on these girls—you'd better make up a list—you know, names and experience—

[SMITTY *takes the list and sits at the table to make some notes.* FLO *takes a look around the room.* DOC *exits Left.*]

FLO. I kinda like the idea of sleepin' in the same room with whole bodies for a change.

SMITTY. If you think it's going to be a picnic keeping them whole, you've got another think coming.

FLO. Not me—I gave up thinkin' a long time ago. Wonder if any of these new kids'll bring a radio that'll pick up the States?

SMITTY. You mean—pick up Montana—don't you?

FLO. Somethin' like that. Last letter I got from Mom was December 6th.

SMITTY. As soon as those Japs find out MacArthur's digging in on the peninsula, none of us will have much time for letters or radios.

FLO. I suppose so. Where's your home, Smitty?

SMITTY. [*After a short pause, looks up.*] I never really had one, Flo. [*Looks back at her work quickly.*]

FLO. Don't talk much about yourself—do ya, fella?

SMITTY. [*Unmistakably changing subject.*] Those kids will be here in a minute—I've got to be ready for them.

FLO. I get it. [*Picking up her gear.*] Make any difference where I stow these?

SMITTY. Help yourself.

FLO. This one's nearest the door— Better take an upper—if they're as green as they look, it might be safer. [*Tosses her stuff on the upper Left bunk at the rear.*] Hmmmm, no wild life—this must have belonged to a General. Oh, Smitty—where's the throne?

SMITTY. Second opening down the line—still giving you trouble?

FLO. Woo-woo.

SMITTY. You never got that paregoric I told you to pick up.

FLO. Couldn't operate without it. Though I haven't decided which is worst. [*Leaning back on bed and stretching luxuriously.*] For the first time the war is what I expected it to be.

[*There are sounds of voices off. The Center door opens and the new recruits stream in. They are:* PAT CONLIN, *a fiery little pug-nosed girl with a good consignment of freckles, who has a bit of swagger about everything she does;* GRACE LAMBERT, *a well-formed and attractive girl of medium height;* HELEN DOMERET, *a lovely statuesque blonde, who carries herself like a model and whose thoughts continually run to men;* NYDIA JOYCE, *a cute little literal-minded Southerner;* SUSAN *and* ANDRA WEST, *auburn-haired English girls*—SUSAN, *the elder, is the leader, continually protecting and looking out for the more fragile* ANDRA; CONSTANCE MARKS, *a Dresden-doll of a girl, beautifully turned out, delicate and, one might think, too fragile for the work ahead. Last is* STEPHANY POLDEN (STEVE), *a large, raw-boned, muscular gal who carries herself like a man. They are all decked out in new uniforms, kits and helmets. Each carries her own extra luggage and they all act as though they were embarking on a pleasure cruise.* NYDIA'S *voice babbles along about "Mosquitoes," etc. as they file into the room and come to a stop.* FLO *and* SMITTY *exchange a look without* FLO'S *whistling coming to a stop.*]

SMITTY. [*Curtly.*] So you're the volunteers?

PAT. That's right, sixteen of us, come over here to help win the war. Who are you?

SMITTY. Smitty's the name.

[*Again the pause.*]

PAT. The other eight had to go right on duty, they—

SMITTY. [*Interrupting.*] I know—right now I'm just interested in who's here. Suppose you each call out your names, and the kind of work you feel yourselves best fitted for. [*To* PAT.] Let's start with you.

PAT. [*With resentment.*] Pat Conlin.

SMITTY. [*Ignoring the antagonism.*] What was your work?

PAT. Lady in waitin'.

HELEN. Oh, Pat!

SMITTY. [*As some of the* GIRLS *snicker.*] Look, Conlin —this isn't a cocktail party you've let yourself in for, and these questions are not intended to be straight lines for a bad comic. We've got to know what you're fitted for so as to be able to do a lot of fighting guys the most good.

PAT. So I was a hash slinger—and I mean *was.*

SMITTY. [*Nods, and notes it on her list. Then to the next girl.*] You?

CONNIE. [*Weakly.*] Constance Marks—I only did welfare work at home, but I want to do anything I can to help.

SMITTY. [*Enters name and looks at* STEVE.] You?

STEVE. Stephany Polden.

SMITTY. P-o-l-d-e-n?

STEVE. Yes. Machine operator in a cannery.

SMITTY. [*Nodding and entering the name.*] Next—

SUE. Susan West—traveling student.

SMITTY. Of what?

SUE. Art.

ANDRA. [*As* SMITTY *looks up at her.*] Andra West—music student.

SMITTY. Sisters?

SUE and ANDRA. Yes.

SMITTY. Next.

[*The next is* NYDIA, *who is much too engrossed in her own affairs to realize she is being called. Both* GRACE *and* HELEN *nudge her. She turns.*]

NYDIA. Oh—present.

SMITTY. [*Patiently.*] What's your name?

NYDIA. Joyce, Nydia—

SMITTY. Any experience Joyce—

NYDIA. Oh, you can call me Nydia.

SMITTY. Swell; what can you do?

NYDIA. Back home where I come from, the women are never allowed to do a blessed thing. But I can knit.

[PAT *lets out a short exclamation of disgust, and* SMITTY *throws her a look.*]

SMITTY. Next.

HELEN. Helen Domeret—P.B.X. switchboard operator.

SMITTY. [*To* GRACE.] And you?

GRACE. Grace Lambert—burlesque—God help me.

SMITTY. [*Smiling.*] This is Flo Harris, you'll be working together. [*Ad lib greetings. Then* SMITTY *continues seriously again.*] You'll find the "Johnnie" in there—next to it, is a store room for extra supplies. At the end's our kitchen. The other door leads into a mobile unit for emergency and overflow from the hospital. Now you'd all better find yourselves a bunk. Doctor Marsh wants to meet you. [*Exits Left.*]

STEVE. [*To* CONNIE, *who looks as if she is going to collapse from fatigue.*] Come on, let me take one of those bags.

CONNIE. [*Smiling wanly.*] Thank you.

STEVE. What's the matter, honey? [*Escorting* CONNIE *toward a bunk.*] Feeling sick again?

CONNIE. A little tired, I'm afraid.

STEVE. [*Crossing down Left.*] I'll get you a glass of water.

CONNIE. Thanks. [CONNIE *continues to her bunk.*] The smell in here is awful, isn't it?

PAT. [*Overhearing her.*] What did you expect it to smell like, a floral shop?

[*The* GIRLS *laugh. They are getting themselves settled.* GRACE *has taken the lower down Right bunk;* HELEN *the upper.* CONNIE *has the lower and* STEVE *the upper Right Center bunk.* SUE *has the upper and* ANDRA *the lower of the bunk Left.* PAT *takes the bunk below* FLO *up Left, leaving the single up Right for* NYDIA.]

HELEN. [*Trying to climb into her upper bunk.*] How are you supposed to get up here?

GRACE. Call the porter I suppose.

PAT. [*To* FLO.] Hey—what did this dump used to be?

FLO. A dump.

PAT. Oh, a wise guy.

FLO. It was a dump—for ammunition—before that, a gun emplacement.

PAT. It's still a dump.

HELEN. From what you've told us about that joint you worked in, you should feel right at home.

GRACE. [*To* FLO.] Say, Harris, have you been with the Army long?

FLO. Since they bombed Nichols Field.

SUE. Nurse?

FLO. For lack of a better word.

HELEN. Any good-looking men to spare up here?

FLO. I don't think you'll be disappointed.

HELEN. It'd be a shame to spoil a good record. [HELEN *starts whistling "Parlez-vous"—then sings, using*

"Battling Battalions of Bataan, parlez-vous—
Battling Battalions of Bataan, parlez-vous—
No Mama—no Papa—no Uncle Sam
But with MacArthur why give a damn—
Hinky-dinky parlez-vous—"

PAT. [*As they start to repeat, yells.*] Hey! Hey! [*Crossing up to Right of bunk where* FLO *sits.*] I hear the Japs have gobbled up most of the islands in the Pacific and are saving us for dessert.

HELEN. You're always hearing things.

GRACE. How does the Intelligence Department manage to get along without you?

PAT. I've had offers—turned 'em down to be where the fireworks are set off.

SUE. [*Coming from her bunk.*] I hope you're right about those fireworks, Pat. I rather want to be on hand when we smash those barbarians.

[SMITTY *enters from Left, closely followed by* DOC. PAT *comes to attention and the other* GIRLS *seeing the older woman, start to get up.*]

SMITTY. Attention all of you. Doctor Marsh.

PAT. Fall in.

[ALL *are tumbling to form ranks.*]

DOC. As you were, girls. You can dispense with the formalities up here. Major Williams has given you your orders, I believe.

PAT. Yes, ma'am, to report to you.

DOC. Good. As he has perhaps told you, we are to operate a Mobile Hospital under his supervision. Theoretically your orders will come from me, but most of the time, you will receive them from Smitty, here. More often than not, the work that you will be called upon to do is distasteful, and you might think it out of your province, but it must be done—the enemy will attempt to dislodge our position as soon as they can bring up their big guns. Anytime now a hell worse than you ever imagined will break loose. As civilian volunteers you still have the right to go back, but for the sake of all those up here who need you, I hope this may never happen. [*Studies their faces for a minute.*] Are there any questions?

NYDIA. Yes, sir—er, I mean, yes, ma'am.

DOC. [*Smiling.*] What is it?

NYDIA. I was just wondering, when do we get our sheets?

DOC. Sheets?

NYDIA. Yes, there isn't even one on my bed, and—

DOC. I'm afraid you'll have to do without a number of things you've never had to before, and sheets are one of the least of them.

NYDIA. Yes, ma'am.

DOC. You'll all have about an hour to get settled here. We'll eat at the hospital tonight at six. Any other questions you have, Smitty or Harris will answer for you. [*She picks up her helmet and bag and starts for the Center door, winking broadly at* SMITTY *as she passes her. In the doorway she turns.*] I can't tell you how glad we are to have you up here. Things were beginning to pile up on us— Good luck.

[*She exits and the* GIRLS *start to return to their bunks.*]

SMITTY. Just a minute, all of you. [*They stop and look at her.*] After mess, Conlin and Domeret will go up to Observation with Harris. She'll show you the ropes, two at a time. The rest of you will come to the hospital with me. And I guess now's as good a time as any to give you a little advice. Until you get to know your way 'round, you'll make things easier for yourselves and everyone else if you stay out of people's way—keep your ears and eyes open and your mouths shut. [*She throws the last at* PAT.] Carry on. [*Turns and exits Right.*]

[GIRLS *return to bunks;* CONNIE *exits Left.*]

PAT. [*With a flip salute.*] Just like that, eh? She didn't waste much time before dishin' out orders.

FLO. Don't get Smitty wrong, she's as square as they come. I've never known her to ask someone to do something she wouldn't do herself.

STEVE. [*Crossing to basin.*] I like her kind. You always know where you stand.

FLO. She grows on you.

PAT. So do warts. I don't think I'm gonna like her.

SUE. Aren't you being rather unfair?

GRACE. Poor Pat's never happy until she's got something to be sore at.

HELEN. [*Who is bouncing on her bunk.*] A night on one of these "third degree" mattresses, and you'll all be sore all over.

FLO. [*Laughing.*] That's what I thought at first, but either you soften them or they harden you, I don't know which.

[ALL *join in the laugh and they settle down to inspecting the place, each girl to her own interest.* NYDIA *is looking for her knitting,* PAT *and* GRACE *are at the table.*]

NYDIA. Well, I like the Doc.

HELEN. She seems regular enough.

GRACE. [*To* FLO.] Yeah, but what does the Doc stand for?

SUE. She is a nurse, isn't she?

FLO. Yep, but she was an important surgeon before she joined the Army.

NYDIA. [*Still searching for her yarn.*] Say, have any of you seen my knitting?

PAT. What are you goin' to do—knit yourself a sheet?

NYDIA. Of course not, silly, it's a sweater for my boy friend—if I can ever find him. We might just as well be in different wars.

HELEN. What is your boy friend, anaemic?

NYDIA. No, he's a bugler with the 43rd. Doesn't it seem funny I haven't been able to find him?

PAT. Not if he knows you as well as we do.

[ALL *laugh at the girl but she continues her search, unconscious of their attention.*]

STEVE. Say, Harris—

FLO. [*Correcting her.*] Flo's the name—

STEVE. Thanks, what is this Observation Smitty mentioned?

PAT. Yeah—what's with the Observation deal—or is it some military secret?

FLO. No, just the Signal Corps Post— The Doc sends us up in shifts to give us a breather. Air raid lookout and field switchboard—

HELEN. [*Suddenly.*] Switchboard!—and I volunteered to get out of a rut.

[CONNIE *screams off Left.* ALL *turn toward the door through which she bursts.* STEVE *catches her.*]

CONNIE. [*In terror.*] Rats—that place is full of rats, we've got to get out of here.

[*The* GIRLS *start to react to* CONNIE'S *terror, but* FLO'S *laugh stops them. They look at her for explanation.*]

FLO. I'm sorry, but things like rats, and sheets won't seem so very important after you get a look at what the boys up in the line and those nurses over in the hospital have to put up with—[*Then, more seriously.*]—and after you've had to write a few letters home for what's left of a man.

[STEVE *takes* CONNIE *to her bunk.*]

PAT. [*After an awkward pause.*] Aw—she ought to be home playin' with her dolls. You don't hear any of the rest of us kickin'.

SUE. We all really do want to do our parts, and we're ever so grateful for your not making us feel horribly green like the others at the Manila hospital, they seemed to forget the time they were green themselves.

FLO. Yeah, I know—I got the works too. I suppose they do get a little tired seein' the surprised looks on each new batch of faces, but most of you will probably find yourselves lookin' on the next batch—if any—in much the same way. [*Suddenly she realizes how serious she is.*] Say—what is this? You've got me goin' like a scratchy record. Suppose I shut up and maybe you'll tell me what's new from the States?

STEVE. Outside of what they did to Manila—all we know is what we hear on the radio, and that ain't much.

FLO. I haven't even seen a radio in days. What do they think over there—what are they doing about all this?

HELEN. You can take it straight from the switchboard —all we're gettin' are rumors.

GRACE. That's right—facts are as rare as our planes in Manila.

FLO. I'll bet they're workin' night and day back home to make up for the mess they've allowed to happen here.

SUE. I'm sure they're all beastly jealous of us being here on the spot. Everyone is simply dying to get their hand in, you know.

HELEN. Yep, they're not havin' much trouble sellin' this war.

ANDRA. That's ridiculous. No one has to sell a war of aggression. I hardly think there is anyone that would sit back and see everything they hold sacred defiled before their very eyes.

PAT. In a pig's ear. I'll bet most of them are afraid they'll have to climb off their plush izzies and shake up their well ordered lives.

HELEN. [*To* FLO, *with a laugh.*] You wanted to know what's goin' on—there you are—both sides of it.

[STEVE *and the* OTHERS *join in on the laugh.* SUE *watches* ANDRA, *who is growing more serious by the minute.*]

ANDRA. Perhaps I'm dense, but I can't see two sides, nor can I see anything frightfully amusing about this war.

[EVERYONE *is stopped short.*]

SUE. [*Fills in the awkward pause.*] What Andra is trying to say is that we are both firm believers that this is a "Holy War" and that any country which turns its back on God can't survive.

PAT. Amen.

[ANDRA *turns on* PAT, *but before she can speak,* NYDIA *jumps up.*]

NYDIA. Why of course—

PAT. [*To* ALL.] See, even Nydia agrees.

NYDIA. I just remembered where I put my knitting.

[ALL *laugh except* ANDRA *and* SUE. *It is not a nasty laugh, but more one of relief.* SUE *sees the trouble is over and starts for the Right door.*]

SUE. I'm rather anxious to have a look around before it turns dark—[*To* FLO.]—think Smitty will object?

FLO. No, but you can go out that way, and ask her—she's inside with some stretcher cases.

SUE. [*Stopping beside* ANDRA.] Like to get some air, Andra?

ANDRA. I'd rather not, if you don't mind.

SUE. Any of the rest of you?

AD LIB. "Are you kiddin' "—"Not me"—"No thanks," etc.

SUE. [*Stops beside* ANDRA.] Sure you don't mind?

ANDRA. Of course not, Susan.

[SUE *starts again for the door up Right.*]

FLO. Hey—[SUE *stops.*]—don't forget your top-hat.

SUE. [*Returns to her bunk and grabs her helmet.*] Righto. [*As she exits Right.*] See you at the hospital. Cheerio.

NYDIA. Ta ta.

HELEN. You and your sister are the walkin'est people I've ever seen.

PAT. [*To* FLO.] Every stop on the way they held us up for a constitutional.

HELEN. I can't imagine working up any more of an appetite. I could eat a horse now.

GRACE. I could put away a couple of hooves myself.

PAT. Better save the gags till after dinner—they probably feed you horse meat up here.

GRACE. I don't care as long as it's stopped buckin'.

[CONNIE *crosses behind table on her way to basin. She carries a towel and cake of scented soap she has taken from her bag.*]

FLO. Don't get too hungry. We can't break for chow till Smitty gets through in there.

PAT. [*Sniffing air and turning to look at* CONNIE.] Phew. What is that? [CONNIE *turns.*] That smell you're usin' should drive out the rats.

STEVE. Leave the kid alone, Pat, she's not botherin' anybody.

PAT. This is a hell of a place to bring perfume.

STEVE. Kinda bad place to bring gripes, isn't it?

PAT. [*Quickly.*] Wait till you get rid of that cold and you'll know what I'm talkin' about.

[*The Center door opens and* SADIE *enters laden with kitchen equipment. She stumbles and some of her pans spill over, making quite a noise.* FLO *rises to greet her.*]

FLO. Sadie— [*Turns to* OTHERS.] Gang, I want you to meet Sadie—the greatest cook in the Army. She can make an inner sole taste like filet-mignon.

AD LIBS. "Hello, Sadie"—"here let me help you"—"when do we eat"—"boy, are we glad to see you."

SADIE. [*After getting her stuff reorganized.*] You'll have to eat at the hospital tonight. Tomorrow I can get things set up here.

[*She exits Left,* FLO *helping her.* NYDIA *and the* OTHERS *seem to have pepped up at the thought of food.*]

NYDIA. Gee—this is going to be fun, isn't it?

HELEN. I'll reserve my opinion till I get a good look at the men.

GRACE. You would.

NYDIA. I wonder where the canteen is?

GRACE. I hardly think they'll have one over here.

NYDIA. Don't be silly—where else do you think they have their dances and shows Saturday night. In every war picture I ever saw there was a canteen.

PAT. Maybe the General didn't see those pictures.

[*There is the distant sound of a SIREN and approaching PLANES.*]

HELEN. What's that?

STEVE. Sounds like an air raid warning.

GRACE. I'll bet it is.

NYDIA. Let's all go out and see. [FLO *enters Left as* NYDIA *starts for the Center door. There is a large EXPLOSION nearby. The lamp shakes.* FLO *watches it sway.*] Maybe we better not.

STEVE. [*To* FLO.] Is it an air raid?

[FLO *nods.*]

PAT. How close is it?

FLO. Too damned close—[SMITTY *enters and crosses to Center door.*]—but you won't have to worry till that lamp starts doin' a Highland Fling.

[ALL *hold a long look at the swaying lamp.*]

SMITTY. Funny time for a raid.

FLO. Yeah.

SMITTY. Probably a flight returning from Clark Field with a few kisses left over.

[*There is another EXPLOSION. All eyes are on the lamp. It only jiggles.*]

FLO. I hope that English girl knows enough to duck.

ANDRA. [*Startled.*] Is there any danger of something happening to her?

SMITTY. No, she's at the hospital by this time.

FLO. Probably.

SMITTY. There go our guns—

[*A new sound is heard, that of ack-ack GUNS.*]

FLO. I was beginning to think those boys at the Observation Battery forgot to wake up.

PAT. They all sound alike to me.

FLO. It won't be long before you'd rather hear that sound than Tommie Dorsey.

CONNIE. [*Tensely.*] What if they drop one here? We'd never get out, would we?

SMITTY. You couldn't be safer in your own bed.

[*The shock of EXPLOSIONS continue, growing more distant.*]

ANDRA. How long does it keep up?

SMITTY. Until they're out of bombs or out of commission.

CONNIE. [*Growing panicky after another SHOCK.*] We've got to get out of here!

SMITTY. [*Seeing this and studying the faces of* ALL.] It's only natural to expect several cases of nerves until you know what this is all about, but we've learned that it doesn't pay to sympathize with crack-ups.

PAT. What makes you think anybody's gonna crack up?

SMITTY. I don't think you'll prove any different from the rest of us.

PAT. You've got a lot to learn.

SMITTY. So I see.

PAT. Just don't take us for a bunch of Patsies.

SMITTY. You might as well take that chip off your shoulder, Conlin. You won't find anyone around here with enough time to knock it off.

[*The SHOCKS have subsided. The PHONE jingles.* SMITTY *goes to it. Again the sound of the SIREN.*]

FLO. Well, the shootin's over, kids.

SMITTY. [*Into phone.*] 63rd Auxiliary, Smith speaking—

STEVE. [*Looking at lamp.*] They come and go fast, don't they?

[*WARN CURTAIN*]

FLO. Sometimes.

SMITTY. Yes, Doc, I understand. See you there. [*Hangs up and turns to* GIRLS.] Well, girls, your baptism's arrived sooner than you bargained for. All that activity you just heard was over at Fort Stotsenberg. We've got to go over there and clean up.

STEVE. Clean up? Are there many hurt?

SMITTY. I'm afraid so.

PAT. Well, come on—what are we waiting for?

[*They* ALL *grab for their tin hats and kits, and pile out Center and up the stairs in a hurry, jabbering as they go.*]

GRACE. [*To* SMITTY.] Will the other girls be there?

SMITTY. No.

HELEN. And they gave us the horse laugh because they got first duty.

AD LIBS. [*As they exit.*] "How about our supper?"
"The hell with supper we can eat any time."
"Don't worry about your sister, kid."
"We'll see her there."
"She can take good care of herself."
"And the other kids thought they'd see action before us—"

FLO. [*Who with* SMITTY, *is preparing more deliberately.*] What a shock they've got coming, and the worst of it is there'll be nothing to replace what they'll lose tonight.

SMITTY. Maybe they're different.

FLO. Who you kiddin'?

SMITTY. [*Has taken a small bottle from her pocket and shaken out a pill which she washes down with a cup of water. Now she turns and starts for the Center door.*] Ready?

FLO. [*As she turns, she shrugs, and tosses her rabbit's foot in the air catching it as it falls.*] Are we ever?

[*They start up the stairs,* FLO *whistling, as the Curtain falls.*]

CURTAIN

ACT ONE

SCENE II

It is eleven-thirty P.M., *four days after the preceding scene.* DOC MARSH *sits at the table working over a pile of reports. At the table beside her,* NYDIA *has dozed off at her knitting. Her hands are on her lap holding a half finished row.* SADIE *is seated on one of the bunks rolling bandages.* ANDRA, *on her bunk, tosses restlessly.* HELEN *on hers sleeps heavily. The rest of the girls are out on duty. There is the sound of distant GUNS.*

AT RISE: DOC *notices a mosquito about to light on* NYDIA'S *face and brushes it off. She smiles a motherly smile at the girl and returns to her work.* GRACE *enters from Right and crosses to the* DOC.

DOC. Yes, Lambert.

GRACE. Everything's ready for that transfusion, Doc Marsh.

DOC. Very good. I'll be right in. [GRACE *exits Right.* DOC *turns to* NYDIA.] Joyce—Joyce, it's after eleven-thirty— [NYDIA *comes out of it and continues her knitting between yawns.*] You and Domeret had better get ready to relieve the Observation detail. [*Exits Right.*]

NYDIA. [*Rising as* DOC *starts out.*] Yes, Doctor. [*Crosses to* HELEN'S *bunk and shakes her.*] Wake up, Helen, we're on duty. [HELEN *grunts and rolls over.*

NYDIA *crosses to her own bunk and puts knitting under pillow.*] Helen.

ANDRA. Please be quiet.

NYDIA. [*Apologetically as she returns to* HELEN.] Oh, I'm sorry. [*More quietly.*] Come on, Helen, you don't want to disappoint the boys.

HELEN. [*Sleepily.*] How about the one I just left?

ANDRA. Will you two shut up?

HELEN. [*Paying no attention.*] Why is it you always wake up from a dream just when it's getting interesting? [*She swings to the floor, yawns and starts to pull on her shoes.*]

[SADIE *puts the bandages on the cabinet and rises.* NYDIA *is getting on her kit.*]

SADIE. [*Going off Left.*] I'll get you both some tea—

HELEN. And a couple of slices of bread—*buttered!* I find it comes up easier that way.

NYDIA. I wonder why I don't get sick like you and Connie?

HELEN. Simple enough— It's all mental.

NYDIA. [*With a blank look.*] Oh, I see.

HELEN. Besides, when you run across a bad one, you pass out before your stomach has a chance.

ANDRA. Shut up.

HELEN. Sounds like they've started up again?

NYDIA. Over an hour ago.

HELEN. Four days and four nights—seems like a year, doesn't it?

NYDIA. I wonder why they're picking on us?

HELEN. They know that General MacArthur can't bring up much in the way of reinforcements while they keep that up.

NYDIA. Can't he?

HELEN. Haven't seen any heavy equipment coming up, have you? [*Starts toward* SADIE *who has entered and is putting tea and sandwiches on table.*] And God knows we need it.

ANDRA. [*Rising up in her bunk.*] Do you two have to make so much noise?

HELEN. You're doing all right yourself.

[SADIE *exits Right.*]

NYDIA. Leave her alone, Helen. I don't think she feels very well.

HELEN. There's nothing wrong with her. [*Looks at* ANDRA *who is pathetically begging silence with a look.*] Why don't you stop dramatizing yourself?

ANDRA. You shut up.

NYDIA. Don't pick on her, Helen. She hasn't slept since Sue disappeared.

HELEN. It makes me sick the way everyone babys her. You'd think she's the only person around here who'd lost something in this war.

ANDRA. [*Rising.*] You nasty beast—you shut up or I'll—

HELEN. Cry for Mama—sure, we know. Isn't there enough grief out here without you loading everybody with your petty troubles?

ANDRA. [*Tense but not hysterical.*] It may be petty to you but I can't stand it—to be around those stinking bodies out there and force myself to help gather up those torn pieces of flesh, and all the while I keep thinking of—of—

NYDIA. Don't, Andra—we understand. [*Looks at* HELEN *and mouths "please."*]

HELEN. I'm sorry, kid—

[DOC *enters Right.*]

ANDRA. [*She doesn't see* DOC.] If only we knew where she is—even if she were—gone, it wouldn't be so bad —but just to disappear— [*She covers her eyes and drops into a chair.*]

DOC. [*Crossing to her.*] I couldn't help overhearing what you just said, West— [ANDRA *looks up.*] No, don't explain—I understand better than you'll ever know. I don't have to think back very far to remember seeing those same planes bombing a town in China. I was helpless to do a thing but watch that death pouring out of the sky. I found myself flat on the ground, pounding it with my fist and bawling like a baby—we can't help that, but we can rise above it. Come on now, on your feet.

ANDRA. [*Rises, unsteadily.*] I'm afraid, I can't stand much more—they keep bringing in more bodies, and not a trace of her—

DOC. [*Evenly.*] There never has been anything pretty about war, West. Men have always destroyed and women have always come along behind and tried to put back the pieces. You know how badly they need you out there now.

ANDRA. [*Breaking to bunk and burying her head in her arms.*] What has all that to do with my sister?

DOC. [*Coldly.*] Perhaps I've been wrong about you. I thought you'd turn out to be one of our best. [*Turns away.*] You don't have to go out with this shift—turn in and try to get some sleep— [*To* OTHERS.] You two had better get started.

NYDIA. Yes, Doctor. [*Exits Center.*]

[DOC *turns from* ANDRA *and sits at table as though she has washed her hands of the girl.* ANDRA *slowly turns and glares at* DOC. HELEN *waits at the table for a last sip.* ANDRA *suddenly straightens and with a look of hatred at the* DOC *moves quickly to her bunk and slips her feet into her shoes. She grabs her kit and helmet and turns toward the door without another look at the* DOC.]

ANDRA. Come on, Helen.

HELEN. [*Without emotion.*] Better reinforce yourself, kid.

ANDRA. I don't want any. Come on. [ANDRA *exits Center.*]

[HELEN *stuffs a sandwich in her pocket and follows her out. As the door closes,* DOC *looks up with a sigh of relief. She smiles to herself and returns to her work. Again the Center door opens and* SMITTY *enters.*]

SMITTY. Greetings, Doc.

DOC. Hello, Smitty, anything new?

SMITTY. Same old story, those babies over there seem to know what we're going to do before we make up our minds.

DOC. They have certainly slowed our communications down to a walk.

SMITTY. It don't add up, Doc. Here they've been raisin' merry hell behind us for five days now, then after a few hours' silence they start hittin' bull's-eyes.

DOC. Lose anybody?

SMITTY. [*Taking a cup of water.*] Stretcher crew.

DOC. [*Worried.*] Not Steve Polden and—

SMITTY. No—a couple of the kids from the village. Never knew what hit 'em.

DOC. [*Relieved, but affected by the loss.*] That's too bad. We needed them. Smitty—

SMITTY. Yes? [*Starts out Right.*]

DOC. Just a minute. I was told something today in the strictest confidence, but I feel if anyone should know —it's you.

SMITTY. Yes?

DOC. Sit down. [SMITTY *sits Center chair.*] Intelligence Headquarters has every reason to believe that someone in the Ambulance Corps is working with a native Fifth Columnist passing on information to the Japs.

SMITTY. One of the girls?

DOC. One of our girls.

SMITTY. I don't believe it.

DOC. We must find her, Smitty. The lives of too many people depend on it.

SMITTY. Do you believe it?

DOC. I'm afraid I do—but it's reassuring to know that after all you've been through—you don't. Found any trace of Sue?

SMITTY. [*Shakes her head.*] Not yet.

DOC. She must have been buried in a fox hole—she couldn't have disappeared.

SMITTY. They're still diggin'.

DOC. Better keep Andra away in case they dig her up.

SMITTY. Yeah, I know.

DOC. Bring in any work for us?

SMITTY. An amputation and a couple of fractures.

DOC. [*Starting out Right.*] Coming?

SMITTY. I'll be right with you. [DOC *exits Right and* SMITTY *wearily rubs her forehead as she crosses to the basin, takes out another pill and washes it down with a cup of water as* CONNIE *enters Right. She is drawn, but does not show the physical signs of the work she's been doing like the rest of the girls. She has managed to keep her uniform neat and her hair brushed. At the moment she is dirty, but she crosses to her bunk and starts to brush off and get her perfumed soap from her bag as* SMITTY *speaks.*] I suppose you've left Polden out there to finish up your work as usual.

CONNIE. It's almost done, and I was afraid I was going to be ill.

SMITTY. How long do you think she'll be able to stay in one piece, doing double duty this way?

CONNIE. Steve doesn't mind, she understands.

SMITTY. What good did you expect to be out here with this constant whimpering and weak stomach of yours?

CONNIE. It's the smell—ether, blood and sweat and that horrible Dakin's solution—I'm all right at Observation.

SMITTY. Who wouldn't be? Sittin' on your can all day pushin' plugs into a switchboard. But every one of the girls needs that breather more than you. You're going to do more of your share around here or give me a better reason than a sensitive nose.

[SMITTY *turns on her heel and starts out Right. As she reaches the door, we can hear the voices of some of the other* GIRLS *approaching.* CONNIE *nervously takes her soap out and crosses to the basin as* GRACE, PAT *and* FLO *enter from Right.* FLO *crosses to her bunk whistling.*]

GRACE. [*Entering.*] Those guys must talk us over like we were a bunch of sheep.

PAT. Nuts. They don't care that much.

GRACE. Well, how else do you think he'd know I have a birth mark on my—

PAT. [*Interrupting.*] Can it. He probably was making a stab in the dark.

FLO. Maybe he caught your act in that burlesque show.

GRACE. It wasn't that *kind* of an act. The way those guys paw you, you'd think they were studying Braille.

[STEVE *enters from Right.*]

FLO. You ought to get on the end of a stretcher. The only boys that come our way aren't interested in birth marks, are they, Steve?

[STEVE *has crossed to* CONNIE *at the basin and ignores* FLO'S *question.*]

STEVE. Feelin' better, honey?

[*She puts her arm around* CONNIE. CONNIE *pulls away self-consciously. The* OTHERS *exchange looks.*]

CONNIE. Yes, thanks.

[CONNIE *is frantically scrubbing her hands.* STEVE *pats* CONNIE *lovingly on the shoulder and moves down to her bunk. The other* GIRL *winks knowingly.*]

GRACE. [*Picking up the conversation.*] Those guys in the fox holes are the worst. They really play rough. We ought to have guns to protect ourselves.

FLO. Nydia's got the right technique.

GRACE. What's that?

FLO. She pretends she doesn't know what they want.

PAT. She's not pretending.

[*They laugh.*]

STEVE. Say, Flo, I think you got in wrong with Helen today.

FLO. Yeah?

STEVE. [*To* GRACE.] One of the boys told Helen she was the loveliest thing he'd ever seen and then Flo marks his chart "Delirious."

FLO. There's only one guy that gets in my hair.

GRACE. Don't tell me, lemme guess—Lieutenant Holt?

FLO. [*Nodding.*] He's a persistent cuss.

GRACE. Somebody's goin' to cool him off one of these days.

STEVE. Smitty's kinda sold on him, isn't she?

PAT. She's not sold on anybody, that piece of ice.

GRACE. Stick around and see the ice melt some time when Lieutenant Holt shows up.

STEVE. I hate to see her waste time on that fellow.

FLO. He's made a pass at every skirt in this outfit.

GRACE. At and under.

[CONNIE *has returned to her bunk after fixing herself carefully before the mirror. She is now getting out her perfume.* GRACE *takes her place at the basin.*]

PAT. I like the guy—at least he puts his cards on the table.

FLO. And how. But it's a pretty worn deck.

GRACE. Poor Pat's been tryin' to get him to walk her and he doesn't even know she's at bat.

PAT. Sour grapes—tchk—tchk. [*She catches sight of* CONNIE *spraying perfume on herself.*] Put on your masks, kiddies, Lady Squeamish is layin' down another gas attack.

CONNIE. [*To* PAT, *sincerely.*] Does this really bother you?

PAT. [*Somewhat disconcerted.*] I can't say I'm nuts about it.

CONNIE. I'm awfully sorry, but it's the only thing that takes that awful smell away. I know that you all put up with a lot from me and I do appreciate it, but please don't begrudge me these little things. They're all I have to remind me of what I've given up.

PAT. Stop, you're killing me. After all, none of us have to stay, you know, so why all the self-pity? There's no reason why you can't act like the rest of us.

STEVE. There are countries where she'd have to act like the rest of them, aren't there, Pat? Yeah and these are the kinda ideas I figured we were all out here fightin' against so we could express ourselves as individuals.

PAT. Aw, you guys are always gettin' serious. Can't a fella have a little fun here without everybody lookin' down his throat to see what made the noise?

GRACE. [*Coming to* PAT'S *assistance.*] You know the only reason we ride Connie is because we're all fed up seeing you do her work every day.

STEVE. [*Quietly.*] I'd do the same for you, Grace—

FLO. Sure, we know it, Steve. We just don't think it's fair, but after all, it's none of our business, so let's stow it; what say?

[PAT *shrugs as* SADIE *enters from Right and crosses toward Left door.*]

GRACE. [*Leaving the basin.*] Hey, Sadie, got anything out there for a bunch of hungry soldiers?

SADIE. In a few minutes now.

GRACE. [*Licking her chops.*] What is it tonight?

PAT. What do you expect, steak and onions?

[SADIE *exits Left, laughing.*]

GRACE. I'll bet that's what they're eating back home.

[SMITTY *dashes in from Right, picks up her kit.*]

SMITTY. Flo—Steve—give me a hand.

[*They are on their way in a rush after* SMITTY *who has exited Center.*]

PAT. [*To* GRACE *as door slams.*] Boy, am I glad I'm not muscular.

GRACE. Your muscles don't show, is all. [*She stoops to pick up some of the cards* STEVE *has knocked off the table in her haste to follow* SMITTY.]

PAT. [*Looking down at* GRACE'S *rear end.*] Maybe not, honey, but yours do.

GRACE. [*Grinning up at her.*] It's all this rich food I've been getting.

PAT. You've sure got a way with Sadie. How's about giving out with the sanzafrance, and gettin' us a good spread for a change?

GRACE. What do you feel like?

PAT. Anything but canned willie.

GRACE. How about some horse au gratin? [GRACE *exits Left.*]

[PAT *becomes conscious of* CONNIE *who is cuddled up in her bunk. She slips down and casually walks to her pulling out a pack of cigarettes.*]

PAT. Cigarette?

CONNIE. [*Looking up surprised.*] No, thanks.

PAT. [*Lighting up.*] What kind of perfume was that you were using?

CONNIE. Mimosa.

PAT. Not so bad once you get used to it.

CONNIE. My favorite.

PAT. I used to go for Jasmine, myself—you know—two bits the jug. [*She holds her hands up to show the size of a gallon jug.*]

CONNIE. [*Grinning despite herself.*] Mother gave me this the night I left.

PAT. Miss home most of all, don't you?

CONNIE. It's not just home so much, as what it stands for.

PAT. We haven't made home stand for much since you got up here, have we?

CONNIE. I can understand the way you feel. I'm sorry I'm such a sissy about things.

PAT. Forget it—we're just jealous is all.

CONNIE. [*Laughing.*] Of me?

PAT. Sure, why not. You're the only one of us that's been honest. You came up here a woman and you've been able to stay feminine. That's what makes the rest of us sore.

CONNIE. You're making fun of me.

PAT. Don't be silly. We're all women, no matter how much we try to pretend we can double for men. We can't and never will. Nature stacked the deck on us. But we've been gnawing our way into men's work until now we've got a mouthful we can't swallow and we're too damned proud to spit it out.

CONNIE. That's very funny telling me that, when I'm so anxious to be like the rest of you.

PAT. The hell with that—stay the way you are—when this is all over you can step back into the groove—what have the rest of us got to look forward to—where'll we ever find the kind of work we've hardened ourselves for—do you think the men we want will take what's left of us?

CONNIE. We'll never live to see the end of this—ever. I'm sure of it now. We'll never leave here alive.

PAT. What are you talking about?

CONNIE. I'm not blind—we can't bring up reinforcements—they've knocked out almost all our air force—pretty soon we'll—

PAT. Cut it out— I happen to know they're expecting to bring in a mess of reinforcements any night now.

CONNIE. Rumors, Pat—they start them to keep us going—we've heard those stories ever since we've come up here.

PAT. This one came right out of old Mac's briefcase—keep it to yourself, kid—'cause I got it from someone little Pat ain't supposed to know—

CONNIE. I'd like to believe it, but—Pat, it's impossible

—we're cut off from everything, there is no way out—we're through—through—

PAT. Ever hear of Cebu?

CONNIE. No.

PAT. Our big island supply base?

CONNIE. You mean?—

PAT. [*Winks and nods.*] Just remember that name.

CONNIE. [PAT *has spoken with such assurance,* CONNIE *seems half convinced.*] Oh, Pat—it would be wonderful, wouldn't it?

PAT. Will be. Come on now, paint on a new face and zitz yourself with a shot of that stink.

CONNIE. Pat, you've been awfully good to—well, to talk to me. I wish there was some way—

PAT. [*Self-conscious.*] Cut it out.

CONNIE. Pat?

PAT. Yeah?

CONNIE. Would you like to use some of my perfume?

PAT. [*Brightens for a moment, then reverts to her old self as she hears* GRACE *enter Center door.*] What the hell are you ravin' about? [PAT *crosses up as the door Center opens.* STEVE *and* FLO *carry the unconscious* ANDRA *in. She relieves* STEVE.] Andra get hit?

[*They put her on her bunk.*]

FLO. Doc just gave her a shot. She was there when they found her sister.

GRACE. You found Sue?

CONNIE. [*Horrified.*] Was she—

FLO. Alive—buried in a fox hole for four days with a half dozen dead bodies.

CONNIE. [*Covering up her eyes.*] Ugh—

STEVE. [*Takes her gently and leads her toward her bunk.*] They'll both be all right, honey.

PAT. [*To* FLO.] Sue must be in a bad way.

FLO. Quiet enough now, but they say she was screaming like a run-over dog until they got her out near the light.

GRACE. Four days in the dark with dead bodies—God.

CONNIE. It's horrible.

[DOC *and* SMITTY *enter from Center leading the whimpering* SUE *who doesn't seem to see anything as she cringes and weakly puts her weight on the two. The* GIRLS *in the room look quietly. She is led out Left.*]

GRACE. [*After an awkward pause.*] Remember the last thing she said that night she walked out of here? [FLO *has covered* ANDRA *and now rises.*] "This is a holy war."

PAT. Talkin' about it's not goin' to help.

SMITTY. [*Entering Left.*] I don't like to do this, but Nydia's been pulled off Observation to replace Andra. Somebody's got to finish out her shift.

CONNIE. Let me.

SMITTY. [*After a pause.*] Go ahead.

STEVE. [*Restraining* CONNIE.] Better let me go, honey. You need the rest.

CONNIE. Not this time, Steve. I want to go. [*Exits Center.*]

PAT. [*To* GRACE.] Where's that food you were goin' to produce?

GRACE. I kinda lost my appetite.

PAT. Aw.

[*She disgustedly starts for the door Left as* DOC *enters.*]

DOC. [*Stops, seeing how affected the* GIRLS *are.*] I know you're all anxious about Sue, but we won't know anything until she recovers from the shock.

STEVE. Sure there's nothing we can do?

DOC. Not a thing.

SMITTY. The other girls will be coming in soon. You'd all better turn in and get some rest.

[*She is looking at* PAT, *who has stopped near the door.*]

PAT. You're setting a swell example.

SMITTY. Just what does that mean?

PAT. Tellin' us to get some rest. Why don't you do it yourself? Tryin' to show us up for a bunch of daisies?

SMITTY. [*Leaning against the Center door.*] I didn't know you were so concerned about my health.

PAT. Don't give me that double talk. You're just flesh and bones like everyone else and when you crack up, don't expect any sympathy from us.

SMITTY. Are you speaking for yourself or all the girls?

PAT. Myself.

SMITTY. That's what I thought. [*She turns into the door and exits.*]

[PAT *kicks the chair.*]

GRACE. Now what was the point of all that? One of these days you'll learn to leave her alone.

FLO. I hope not, it's a lotta fun to watch.

STEVE. As long as you don't bring the rest of us into your feud.

FLO. Let her spout, Steve. The Irish never give you any trouble as long as they're talkin'. It's when they're corked up you got to keep an eye on 'em.

PAT. So we're all supposed to get some rest with that racket out there? [*Indicates outside.*] She can't rest herself's why she puts on this superwoman act to cover it up.

NYDIA. [*Entering Right on the end of this.*] Who?

PAT. Eleanor. [*Crosses to door Center, opens it a crack and looks out.*]

NYDIA. [*To* OTHERS.] Oh, is she out here now?

FLO. [*To* NYDIA.] You off duty already?

NYDIA. Yes, everything's quiet inside.

GRACE. Maybe I'd better move my bunk in there.

FLO. [*Crawling into her bunk.*] You'd be safe.

GRACE. [*Who has climbed into her bunk.*] And maybe get a little rest.

NYDIA. [*Taking out her knitting.*] Oh, no you wouldn't. That boy in number seven's never still a minute.

STEVE. [*Sitting on her bunk.*] What's that you're makin', honey?

NYDIA. That sweater—for my boy friend. [*Holds it up. It's tremendous.*] See, I've almost got the back finished.

GRACE. [*Poking her head out of her bunk.*] What a man.

NYDIA. [*Surprised.*] Oh, do you know him?

GRACE. Go to sleep.

NYDIA. I want to finish this row.

GRACE. [*Sleepily.*] Don't rattle your needles or we won't be able to hear the guns.

NYDIA. [*With a childish chuckle.*] Silly.

[STEVE *seems impervious to everything already.* GRACE *slowly dozes off and* NYDIA'S *knitting grows slower and slower until she dozes in the middle of a stitch.* FLO *is on her bunk reading a letter.* PAT *closes door and crosses to* FLO'S *bunk.*]

PAT. [*Quietly to* FLO.] I don't see how they can drop off like that. [FLO *doesn't answer.*] I can catch forty winks out there—but in here— [*Shakes her head and takes a look at* FLO *who nods and continues with her letter.*] You know, I've caught myself workin' and sleepin' at the same time, lately. I've come out of it several times and found myself finishin' a bandage I couldn't remember ever startin'.

FLO. I've done that. Funny feeling, isn't it?

PAT. Yeah, wonder why I can relax out there and get all tied in knots in here.

FLO. Cloisterphobia.

PAT. Nuts. [*Exits Left.*]

[*The door Center opens and* HELEN *enters, waves wearily to* FLO. *She crosses to her bunk and deposits her helmet and kit. She takes towel and soap and crosses to basin. Quietly to* FLO.]

HELEN. Letter. [FLO *nods.*] Don't it make you homesick?

FLO. I suppose so. Kinda nice, though.

HELEN. I guess I don't know enough people who can write— [FLO *smiles and returns to her letter. After a moment* HELEN *continues.*] Where's your home, Flo?

FLO. Oh, just a little jerk-water town in the Northwest. Why?

HELEN. Farm country?

FLO. [*Thinking—her eyes looking off.*] Cherries and apples—

[*There is a pause.*]

HELEN. I could go for an apple right now.

FLO. So could I. Did you ever pick a yellow-red Milden off the tree in early winter and bury your teeth in it—you can hear it snap as the juice gushes into your mouth.

HELEN. [*Watching her.*] I've never even seen an apple tree.

FLO. [*Smiling, almost lost in her memories.*] They were always sweeter in the upper orchard. I guess because Mom never let us go up there when we were kids. She used to say if we were goin' to break our necks fallin' out of trees, we might as well do it near the house.

HELEN. [*Looking off.*] The only apples I ever picked were off old Tony's cart over on Second Avenue. They were always red on top and black underneath, and the only thing that ever snapped at us were the worms inside.

FLO. You'd like Mom. Kinda old-fashioned, but gosh, can she cook.

HELEN. [*Moved.*] I'd like to meet her some day.

[*A sudden SHOCK rocks the room. The light flickers.* STEVE, GRACE *and* NYDIA *all swing upright in their bunks and look at the lamp.*]

PAT [*Rushing in Left.*] Air raid.

[*Almost as she speaks the sound of the warning SIREN starts to howl in the distance, followed by another SHOCK.*]

HELEN. Boy, that's not far away.

[*From now until the Curtain, these SHOCKS continue at irregular intervals.*]

GRACE. Those yellow sons of billy-goats must've known I was asleep.

NYDIA. What could they be after at this hour?

PAT. Some natives probably left their fires burning again.

HELEN. [*Stopping by* ANDRA.] How can she sleep after that last one?

FLO. With all the morphine they shot in her she could sleep through the burnin' of Tokio.

GRACE. The lucky stiff.

STEVE. Sounds like a bad one.

PAT. There's one consolation. Nothin' can top the mess we got into that first night.

CONNIE. [*The door Center opens quickly and* CONNIE *scurries in, slamming the door behind her. She is breathless, her eyes wide with fear.*] The hospital!

[*WARN CURTAIN*]

[DOC *and* SMITTY *enter Right.*]

DOC. The hospital?

CONNIE. Yes, there must be fifty of them up there. The first bomb was a direct hit and now the whole hospital's in flames.

DOC. [*Badly shaken.*] They knew it was a hospital. They've been flying over here for weeks.

CONNIE. They just keep diving down and dropping one after another into what's left of it.

[PAT *makes a break for the Center door.* DOC *stops her.*]

DOC. Where do you think you're going?

PAT. Why stand here gassing when we might do some good out there.

DOC. Without your helmet or kit? There are enough dead heroes out there now. [*To* OTHERS.] Inside all of you—two to a stretcher—double your kits and Smitty will provide you with what you'll need. Keep your heads! [DOC *watches them start out Right. Grimly to herself.*] You're nurses now. [*As* SMITTY *is about to leave.*] Smitty— [SMITTY *stops*—DOC *picks up her kit and starts for Center door.*] Keep them here until this is over.

SMITTY. You're not goin' out there—

DOC. That's my job.

SMITTY. Let me go—

DOC. [*Indicates other room.*] They're your job—and it's a big one. [*Starts up Center steps.*]

SMITTY. Watch yourself— [DOC *winks and exits Center.*] God—I've never bothered you much—but please keep an eye on her.

CURTAIN

ACT TWO

SCENE: *Late afternoon, several days later. There is the distant sound of PLANES and a feeble BARRAGE which keeps them high.* PAT *enters the empty stage from Right, carrying a folded, blood-stained stretcher. She is near the point of exhaustion.* HELEN *follows a few steps behind her and tries to wipe from her eyes the scene she has just left.* PAT *steadies herself against the table.*

PAT. Christ—what butchery—

HELEN. When does this let up—when are they going to relieve us—God—I can't go out there again.

PAT. Stick it, kid—there are only eight of us now to do what they figured was too much for sixteen.

HELEN. [*Shaking badly.*] What good does it do—what we've been bringin' in would be better off dead.

PAT. [*Refilling her kit with bandages.*] Comin'?

SMITTY. [*At that moment* SMITTY *enters hurriedly from Center, sees the* GIRLS *as she moves to the medicine kit. To* PAT.] Keep moving.

PAT. [*Starting for Right door.*] Aaaa—

HELEN. [*Shakes herself out of her fog and stumbles toward the Center door. To* SMITTY.] The Doc can't handle another in there—

SMITTY. [*Shortly.*] I know—they're taking everything else alive back to Mariveles Bay—they need hands.

[HELEN *exits Center.* PAT *turns to* SMITTY.]

PAT. Geez, but you're a big brave girl— [*Exits Right letting the door slam.*]

[SMITTY *looks for a minute after them and then starts to lay out her surgical kit at* GRACE'S *bunk.* DOC *enters Right, taking off a badly smeared apron.*]

DOC. Glad you're here, Smitty—how's Grace?

SMITTY. [*Still affected by* PAT'S *words.*] Piece of shrapnel in the leg. Steve's helping her in.

DOC. How are the girls holding up?

SMITTY. Damn it, Doc—they came up here to wrap bandages and run switchboards—they're not nurses, let alone undertakers. We've no right to let them go out there.

DOC. Now that Major Williams and his staff at the hospital are gone—we haven't much choice.

SMITTY. They can't keep going—they've got to let up or crack up.

DOC. [*Filling her kit with supplies; quietly.*] What do you propose doing, Smitty?

SMITTY. [*Relenting with a sigh.*] If I knew, I suppose I'd do it instead of popping off.

DOC. They'll come through.

SMITTY. After this, nobody'll have the nerve to suspect any of them of working for the Japs.

DOC. [*Seriously.*] A patrol shot the native this morning trying to slip through the lines—one of the girls in our uniform was there but got away.

SMITTY. It's a rotten lie, Doc—not one of our girls would—

DOC. [*Interrupting.*] This is no time for sentiment, Smitty. She's got to be stopped! [*Exits Center.*]

[SMITTY *crosses to basin wearily. The door Center opens and* GRACE *enters, supported by* STEVE. GRACE'S *face is somewhat flushed and her speech indicates the pain she is suffering.* SMITTY *helps get* GRACE *into her bunk.*]

SMITTY. Lose much blood?

GRACE. Couple of jiggers, I guess.

SMITTY. [*To* STEVE.] Steve, you'd better take a look at Sue. [*Cuts dirty bandage from* GRACE'S *leg as* STEVE *exits Left.*] Hurt much?

GRACE. Burns, mostly. [*Trying to sit up and see.*] How does it look?

SMITTY. [*Pushing her down.*] Not bad. How's Andra holding up?

GRACE. Gee, she's a different person—she can't seem to get enough of— [SMITTY *is probing the wound to locate the piece of shrapnel.*] *Jesus!* what are you doing? [*Tries to sit up again and* SMITTY *shoves her back roughly.*]

SMITTY. Keep your head down—if you'd done that out there, this wouldn't have happened.

GRACE. [*Resentfully.*] That's a swell thing to say—

SMITTY. [*Taking up a pair of forceps.*] You had plenty of warning, why weren't you under cover?

GRACE. [*Rising to the bait.*] You don't think I was out there for laughs, do you?

SMITTY. [*Snapping right back.*] You're not going to be much use on crutches, you know.

GRACE. You've got just about as much heart as—

[*Just as* GRACE *loses her temper and is about to shout,* SMITTY *reaches in her wound and extracts the shrapnel buried there. She pulls it out and* GRACE *finishes her speech in a shrill scream.*]

SMITTY. [*To distract her.*] You're right, it doesn't pay to have a heart in this work. [*Starts swabbing and bandaging the leg.*]

GRACE. [*Really in pain, fighting back with words.*] You've got a heart all right—for Lieutenant Holt.

SMITTY. [*Stung.*] You've got a fever.

GRACE. And you wear it on your sleeve.

SMITTY. You'd better cut that out.

GRACE. [*Following up her advantage.*] It's hardly a secret—so there is something the great Smitty can't take—[*Tauntingly.*]—and he doesn't give a damn for you.

SMITTY. [*Rising and snapping her kit closed.*] Shut up.

GRACE. [*Speaking rapidly.*] He's a rat. [SMITTY *raises her hand as though she were going to strike* GRACE, *then stops, picks up her kit and moves rapidly to the door Right. She is livid.*] He makes passes at every girl he gets alone— [SMITTY *exits.* GRACE *shouts after her.*] Ask any of the girls—just ask them. Ask them. [*She drops on her elbow weakly.*]

STEVE. [*Enters Left and sees that* GRACE *is shaking. She crosses quickly and puts her arm around her.*] Don't get all riled up, baby—

GRACE. [*Shaking* STEVE *off.*] Leave me alone.

STEVE. [*Stroking her head.*] You've got a fever, honey. Now just relax and let Steve take care of you.

GRACE. Take your big hands off me—you can't paw me like you do Connie.

STEVE. [*Believes her sicker than she really is.*] Easy, easy, honey—come on now, let's get those clothes off—I'll help you—

GRACE. [*Struggling.*] Take your hands off me, I tell you. Go maul your Connie.

STEVE. [*Realizing* GRACE *means trouble.*] What's bothérin' you, honey?

GRACE. Honey, hell—take your paws off me. [*She pushes* STEVE *off balance and the girl falls to the floor.*] Always wantin' to put your arms around people—callin' 'em "Honey" and strokin' their hair—why don't you go out there and fight with the rest of the men—you—you Freak! [STEVE *is stunned. After a moment she gets up stiffly, looking into* GRACE'S *face, unable to believe what she's heard. Slowly the meaning of the accusation hits her.* GRACE *is sobered by the effect of her words on* STEVE. *She stares at* STEVE'S *hurt face as the girl turns and slowly moves up and out the door Center.* SADIE *enters Left as she is leaving.* GRACE *calling after her.*] Steve—Steve. Come back here—it's not true, come here.

SADIE. [*Crossing to* GRACE.] What's the matter?

GRACE. [*Frantically.*] Stop her.

SADIE. Stop her?

GRACE. Get Steve, I tell you. Tell her I didn't know what I was saying. Tell her anything, but make her come back.

[SADIE *is puzzled, but hurries out Center to get* STEVE. PAT *and* NYDIA *enter from Right.*]

PAT. [*To* GRACE.] Well, how's the old campaigner?

GRACE. [*In tears.*] I wish I were dead.

PAT. You came near enough that a little while ago—

GRACE. [*Miserable.*] Leave me alone.

PAT. [*Hurt.*] Nothing I can do?

GRACE. No.

PAT. Sorry.

NYDIA. [*Crosses down Right.*] Gee, Grace— [PAT *stops her with a warning gesture.*] Gosh, I didn't know it was that bad.

[*She tiptoes back to her bunk as* PAT *exits Left.*]

SADIE. [*Enters Center.*] Grace? [GRACE *turns over and looks up hopefully.*] I told her what you said—

GRACE. Yes?

SADIE. She just mumbles, "I ain't sore at her," and walks off. What—

GRACE. Thanks, Sadie, forget about it, will you?

SADIE. [*Shrugging.*] Sure. [*She moves off Left.*]

NYDIA. [*Tiptoes back to* GRACE'S *bunk.*] Gosh, Grace, the way you acted I thought you were dying—

GRACE. I'm all right.

NYDIA. Oh, sure. [*Cocking her head on one side.*] But I'll bet it hurts a lot.

GRACE. [*Wanting to preclude conversation.*] It's just numb, you ought to understand.

NYDIA. [*Brightly.*] Of course, I knew a woman once who had her arm cut off in an auto accident and it was so numb she didn't know it until she reached for her hankie.

GRACE. Why don't you get back to your knitting?

NYDIA. [*A little hurt.*] All right, only I thought you might like someone to talk to and cheer you up.

GRACE. Thanks, I'll pull through— [*She rolls over again.* NYDIA *moves away.*] I'll call you when I need a hankie.

SMITTY. [*Returns from Right, sees* NYDIA.] Oh, Nydia, while you're up—

NYDIA. Yes?

SMITTY. [*Taking a bedpan from the wall near basin.*] See what you can do for that fellow in number five.

NYDIA. Aw— [*She moves up, takes the bedpan and exits Right.*]

[*The door Center opens before* NYDIA *exits.* STEVE, ANDRA *and* FLO *enter, supporting a* NATIVE WOMAN *who is heavy with child and obviously in labor.* CONNIE *enters behind them and closes the door.*]

SMITTY. Who is she?

ANDRA. [*She is a completely different girl, self-possessed and hard as steel. The shock has brought her around.*] One of the villagers—tried to get back through the lines during the last raid. Steve found her.

FLO. She's in labor.

NYDIA. [*Staring at her.*] She doesn't look underfed like the others.

SMITTY. Go on, get going.

NYDIA. I wish I'd stayed at home.

[SMITTY *relieves* STEVE. FLO, CONNIE *and* PAT, *who has re-entered, help.* STEVE *seems still dazed as she watches them go off Left. She turns around, sees* GRACE *and moves toward her.*]

GRACE. You've got to believe me, Steve, I didn't know what I was saying.

STEVE. [*Interrupting, speaking as though in a trance.*] You shouldn't have said what you did—

GRACE. I didn't know what I was saying. I couldn't—

STEVE. [*Interrupting again.*] Do the other girls say those things about me?

GRACE. Of course not, Steve, it doesn't make sense.

STEVE. Pat does, doesn't she?

GRACE. Honestly Steve, it was my leg, and you were there just when I didn't want anything more to touch me—

STEVE. Do they really call me a—a—

GRACE. Please stop talking like that, the whole thing's ridiculous.

STEVE. [*Moving as though to leave.*] You shouldn't have said what you did—

NYDIA. [*Entering Right all of a dither.*] Steve, come and give me a hand, will you?

[STEVE *without a word starts after* NYDIA *off Right.* FLO, ANDRA *and* PAT *return.*]

ANDRA. [*Speaking as she enters.*] I've got to get back—

PAT. I'd like to get hold of the bottle you found your energy in.

ANDRA. I can't help feeling there's so little time and I'm not all done in, really.

FLO. What are you going to do, pass up now?

PAT. Sure. Why go out now? We'll be eatin' in half an hour.

ANDRA. I'll be back for chow. There's a gunner up there who's going to show me how to operate his anti-aircraft gun. He's brought down seven himself. It's one of the things Sue would have done—[*More thoughtfully.*]—if she'd had a chance— [*Starts out Center.*]

FLO. [*After a pause.*] Take care of yourself.

ANDRA. Don't worry, I'm beginning to like this war. [*Exits Center.*]

PAT. [*Crossing to her bunk.*] Wants to fire a gun and only yesterday she was cryin' for Mama.

FLO. It's hard to look at Sue without wanting to kill.

PAT. [*In an awed tone.*] You know, I don't get her, the way she screams at night, and looks at you without seemin' to see.

FLO. Doc says it'll take months, maybe years, before the effect of the shock'll wear off.

PAT. They're really goin' to send her back to Cab Cabin.

FLO. The first lull in this everlasting bombardment.

GRACE. [*Coming out of her silence.*] Do you think they might send me back?

PAT. [*Sarcastically.*] I suppose if you wanted to bad enough.

GRACE. Smitty said I wouldn't be much good to anybody.

PAT. You sure sound anxious.

FLO. Aren't we all, really?

PAT. I'm not, I hate those bandy-legged bastards a little better every day.

GRACE. [*To* PAT.] You're sore at me, aren't you, Pat?

PAT. Who's sore?

GRACE. I didn't mean to be short with you a little while ago.

PAT. [*Mollified.*] Forget it—still hurt?

GRACE. Oh, it's not bad—why aren't you in there with Smitty?

PAT. The woman's about ready to have her baby. I suppose they figured too many cooks might spoil the birth—

GRACE. Corn.

FLO. Did you notice the way Connie shoved me out of the way and went right to work with Smitty in there as though she loved it?

PAT. Why not, it's the first woman's job she's had a chance to do up here.

FLO. I'd like to see it happen. I've watched cows and horses, but I've never seen a baby.

PAT. Aw, I'm just as glad, I'm gettin' tired of watchin' Smitty strut her stuff. [FLO *chuckles.*] Think it's funny?

FLO. It wasn't that. I was just wonderin' what the Creator was thinkin' of when he decided to light that little candle in there in the midst of this hurricane.

[*There is the plaintive CRY of a baby in the room Left. The* GIRLS *all look off.*]

PAT. It's a girl.

FLO. How do you know?

PAT. By its voice of course.

FLO. You sound like Nydia. [*Starts toward her bunk.*]

PAT. Going in?

FLO. No, just remembered we left all our stuff out there when Steve called us. [CONNIE *enters from Left. She is looking better than she has for some time.*] Is it over?

CONNIE. [*Going to the basin and washing.*] It's a boy— [*They look at* PAT *and laugh.*] The mother died. [*She turns to the basin as the laugh dies suddenly.*]

FLO. [*After a pause.*] She wanted so badly to have the kid in her own place.

GRACE. Know who she was? [CONNIE *shakes her head.*] Sorta makes the baby ours, doesn't it?

PAT. And another grave to dig.

CONNIE. [*Crossing to bunk. a little annoyed.*] I suppose that's one way of looking at it.

SMITTY. [*Enters from Left. She is rubbing her hands on a towel.*] Flo, will you see what you can do in the kitchen, Sadie's way behind with all these interruptions.

PAT. I'll do it. Flo's got to gather up her stuff outside. [*Starts out Left.*]

GRACE. Oh, Pat, give me a hand and I'll help.

SMITTY. [*Sharply.*] Okay, but keep your weight off that leg. [PAT *goes back to give* GRACE *a lift as* FLO *starts out Center.* NYDIA *enters looking very peaked.* SMITTY *to* FLO.] You'd better take Connie and Nydia with you, they both look as if they could use a little air.

[CONNIE *picks up her helmet where she dropped it when she came in.*]

FLO. Come on, Nydia.

NYDIA. [*Getting her helmet from her bunk.*] Coming.

[CONNIE *passes* SMITTY *as she joins* FLO *at the Center door.*]

SMITTY. Thanks for the help in there, Connie.

[*She moves over to the desk as* CONNIE *almost gives her a double take.* PAT, *who is lifting* GRACE *from her bunk, also turns at* SMITTY'S *remark.*]

NYDIA. [*Moves to join* FLO *and* CONNIE *at the Center door.*] Where are we going?

FLO. To pick some flowers for chow. [*Holds the door open.*]

NYDIA. Gosh, are we all out of food?

FLO. [*As she closes the door.*] Come on.

[PAT *has* GRACE *on her feet.*]

PAT. This'll take your mind off Lieutenant Holt for a while.

GRACE. And give Helen the break she's been waitin' for—

PAT. She's no competition—too obvious— Hey— [*As* GRACE *winces.*] Take it easy—doesn't it hurt?

GRACE. Feels like there's a hot poker in there, but aside from that, it's wonderful.

PAT. With all they had to shoot at, how could they hit your leg?

GRACE. It was the best looking leg out there, wasn't it?

[*They exit Left.* SMITTY *sits at table and starts work on papers.* STEVE *slowly enters Right.*]

SMITTY. What's the matter, Steve, or is it just tired?

STEVE. [*Looking at* SMITTY, *then at the basin.*] I suppose I am—kinda. Smitty, did the woman pull through?

[STEVE *starts to wash and* SMITTY *leans against the wall near the basin watching her.*]

SMITTY. No.

STEVE. I figured she wouldn't.

SMITTY. Her son's in there, though, very much alive. You ought to take a peek.

STEVE. [*Doesn't answer for a moment. She takes a towel and turns to* SMITTY. *Her voice is uncertain when she speaks.*] You're a straight shooter, Smitty. I don't suppose you'd lie to me—that is, if I wanted the truth—would you?

SMITTY. Get it off your chest, Steve.

[STEVE *moves to up Right corner of table before she speaks again.* SMITTY *takes out a pack of cigarettes and moves down Left of* STEVE *and offers her one.* STEVE *shakes her head. She starts to speak as* SMITTY *lights up.*]

STEVE. I don't know much about life—I suppose, the way I was brought up in a lumber camp. Nobody had much schoolin' but everything was honest and above board. [*She pauses to collect her words.*] Men were—well, just men, and the women raised kids and there was never any mystery about sex. [*She pauses again.*] I've picked up a lot since I grew out of that life and some things I don't understand. I—well—I— [*She gags on what she is trying to get out and moves down toward her bunk.*] It's no use, Smitty, I just can't get it out. I thought I could, to you, but I just can't.

SMITTY. [*She follows* STEVE *to the bunk.*] Some of the girls been makin' cracks?

STEVE. Is there anything wrong with me, Smitty? Am I different from them, Smitty? [SMITTY *hesitates and* STEVE *mistakes her pause for embarrassment.*] Tell me honest, Smitty, I gotta find out. I'm so confused.

SMITTY. If there was anything wrong with you—anything to be ashamed of, you'd know it. You'd know it here, Steve—[*Touches her heart.*]—long before anybody else.

STEVE. But I don't, Smitty. I've never even thought—

SMITTY. [*Interrupting.*] And you mustn't. Right now you're confused—hurt— Cancers grow from that kind of hurt, Steve— It's a word that's hit you below the belt—shake it off while it's still a word, Steve, because accepting it makes it real and gives it a chance to grow. There are enough lies out there—[*Indicates outside.*] —kicking hell out of decent things without letting one of them tear you apart.

STEVE. [*With more control.*] I know it, and yet—it's got me so mixed up.

SMITTY. You can handle it— [STEVE *smiles back at* SMITTY *and reaches out involuntarily to squeeze* SMITTY'S *hand. Suddenly she self-consciously realizes* GRACE'S *words and withdraws the hand.* SMITTY *takes the hand before the girl can completely withdraw it. She holds it firmly.* SADIE *has entered with a tray of utensils and is now busy setting the table.*] Something smells good out there, Sadie.

SADIE. It's rice again, I'm sorry, but—

SMITTY. [*Crosses to table.*] It still smells good. How did you ever pull yourself away from that baby?

SADIE. He's sleepin' like an angel—fell asleep with his tiny hand around my little finger.

SMITTY. [*Turning back to* STEVE.] Steve, you'd better show a little interest in that baby before you hurt Sadie's feelings.

SADIE. [*All for leaving the table and taking* STEVE *in.*] The sweetest little thing you ever saw. Come on, I'll show you.

SMITTY. Steve can find the way, and we want our supper.

[STEVE *exits Left. There is a sudden SHOCK, and the lamp jiggles and flickers. The SIREN sounds and another SHOCK makes the lamp jump. The door Center opens and* CONNIE, FLO, HELEN *and* NYDIA *tumble in, covered with dirt.*]

FLO. Whew, that was the closest yet.

NYDIA. They make me so mad. Why, they could easily have killed us.

[*They are* ALL *dusting themselves off.*]

HELEN. We heard them coming even before the warning. They were trying to get the Observation Battery. One of the bombers just exploded in the sky—blew into a million pieces like a toy balloon—what a sight.

CONNIE. [*Crosses to basin.*] It was horrible.

HELEN. I thought it was beautiful.

SADIE. [*Who has rushed through her work.*] Helen, I've got something to show you.

HELEN. I can smell it.

SADIE. Not this surprise. Come on—

HELEN. I'll be out in a minute. [SADIE *exits Left.* HELEN *turns to* NYDIA *beside her.*] I wonder what it is.

NYDIA. Probably something one of the boys gave her.

FLO. No, it's the baby I was telling you about when the fun started outside.

HELEN. [*More excited.*] Oh, sure—I'd forgotten—come on, let's have a look.

NYDIA. [*To* FLO.] What's his name?

FLO. [*From her bunk.*] We haven't gotten around to askin' him yet.

NYDIA. He's got to have a name.

[*She and* HELEN *exit Left.*]

FLO. [*To* CONNIE *who is crossing to her bunk.*] Sometimes, I don't think she knows there's a war goin' on.

SMITTY. [*Takes up phone.*] Give me R95— [SADIE *enters with bread, plates and other things for the table. She sets them in place as* SMITTY *waits.*] Hello—this is Smitty, Doctor Marsh there? [*The answer seems to relieve* SMITTY.] Swell. Thanks— No, don't bother her, I was afraid she might have been caught in the raid—

[SMITTY *hangs up and exits Left as we hear the voices of* HELEN, PAT, *and* NYDIA *coming back.*]

NYDIA. I think we ought to give him a good Christian name.

PAT. Like Messer-Schmidt.

[HELEN *sits at table,* NYDIA *continues to her bunk where she drops wearily.* PAT *stops Center.* SADIE *exits Left.*]

NYDIA. [*Repeating as though familiar.*] Messer-Schmidt —yes, French names are always cute—

HELEN. How about Adam—our first man.

NYDIA. I don't like it.

HELEN. And I'm too tired to argue.

NYDIA. [*Stretching out.*] Gosh, this feels good.

HELEN. Funny isn't it, the more tired you get the more you think of men.

FLO. You know, Helen, with your interest in men, you ought to make a swell nurse.

PAT. [*Working around the table.*] She's not interested in the kind that need a nurse.

HELEN. I'm beginning to believe that the guys in one piece out there need more attention than the ones who've been cut down.

NYDIA. Helen, you shouldn't talk that way, somebody's liable to misunderstand you.

HELEN. [*Laughing wearily.*] Only you, baby—only you.

[SADIE *enters Left with steaming pot.*]

PAT. Food. [*Sitting down.* HELEN *is already serving herself.*] Gather round, kiddies, we won't wait for Helen.

HELEN. I never get too tired to eat.

FLO. Come on, you two.

AD LIBS. Rice again—and carabao stew—rice and salmon —rice and rice— Come on, Nydia.

NYDIA. [*Coming to table.*] What are we having?

PAT. Rice.

NYDIA. We had that last night. [*The* GIRLS *slowly gather at the table, taking seats at random. They start helping themselves immediately.* STEVE *returns and hesitates, then decides against sitting. She exits up Right.* GRACE *enters on crutches too short for her. To* GRACE.] Now you even look like a cripple.

GRACE. These things must have been tailored for La-Guardia. [*They laugh as she awkwardly navigates to the table and sits.*] Say, I hear you kids nearly got it out there.

HELEN. We just made it by the skin of our teeth.

NYDIA. The biggest plane you ever saw.

FLO. Looked like they got it from Observation.

PAT. Helen, you were on Observation today, weren't you?

HELEN. [*Mouth full.*] Yep—

PAT. Hear anything interesting?

HELEN. All the time I was on Old Ramrod was burning up the wires to Corregidor. Didn't have much chance to listen in, though.

FLO. [*Calling off Left.*] Sadie, how about some more bread.

SADIE. [*Off.*] Sure.

[SMITTY *has entered from Left.* PAT, *whose back is to her, doesn't see her.*]

PAT. Didn't you hear anything about reinforcements we're supposed to be gettin'?

HELEN. [*Seeing* SMITTY, *whose face is a mask.*] Not much.

PAT. [*Sees* HELEN *look behind her and turns to face* SMITTY. *Sarcastically.*] Oh, I forgot. Switchboard operators aren't supposed to repeat conversations they overhear while on duty—especially when snoopers are around.

SMITTY. [*Sitting.*] It's a good rule to remember.

PAT. Why do we have to play these games among ourselves? We all know they've been trying to bring up mechanized units, and haven't been able.

SMITTY. You should know by now there's a reason when we're told to do things up here.

PAT. Always lookin' for an excuse to ride me.

GRACE. Poor little Pat—

ANDRA. [*The door Center bursts open and* ANDRA *enters, a dirty picture of glowing animation. Excitedly.*] Any of you see it?

HELEN. What?

ANDRA. The plane, did any of you see it come down?

GRACE. Who gave you the shot in the arm?

ANDRA. [*The words tumbling out.*] In that last raid—they got Bill, the gunner at Observation—he was showing me how to operate—I was standing beside him when he fell— Before I knew it, I had taken his place—I just pointed the gun at the biggest one that was coming right at us, and held the trigger—suddenly it crumpled in the air and burst into flames—

PAT. [*Crossing to her.*] Come again.

GRACE. But slower.

SMITTY. [*Incredulous.*] You mean—you brought down a plane?

ANDRA. Rather!—George, the other gunner, said it was the one that did for Bill. I wish I'd been able to get another.

[*The* GIRLS *have crowded around* ANDRA, *and are shouting congratulations and patting her on the back.*]

FLO. Honest.

HELEN. Gee, that's marvelous.

PAT. Well, you lucky stiff.

CONNIE. [*Interrupting the spell.*] How can you be proud of a thing like that?

ANDRA. [*Quickly and with much feeling.*] I've never been more proud of anything in my life.

[*There are more ad libs of agreement during which* CONNIE *takes her plate and retires to her bunk alone.*]

SMITTY. [*Crossing to* ANDRA.] It might not be a good idea to let Headquarters hear about it, but—[*Sticks out her hand.*]—unofficially, I envy you.

HELEN. [*Who has been frantically searching her bag, pulls out a bottle of brandy and returns to the table.*] Something told me to save this for an occasion— [HELEN *crosses and starts to pour a few drops into the cups.*]

PAT. [*Helps by pouring out water or coffee into the bowl in the center of the table.*] Brandy—tchk—tchk—

FLO. Where did you find it?

HELEN. I've always been afraid of snakes.

NYDIA. [*Smelling it.*] Umm, smells like plum pudding—

[*Ad libs—"Quiet, quiet"—"Come on, Andra."*]

GRACE. Tell us more.

ANDRA. [*Reveling in it.*] George said I've got a swell eye. Of course it was only beginner's luck.

PAT. You know you don't believe that. [*Holding up her cup, starting to sing; others join in.*] Here's to Andra, she's true blue, she's a soldier through and through—

when she dies you'll hear them say—if she doesn't go to heaven she'll go the other way—so drink, chugalug—chugalug chugalug—

[*They keep singing "drink" and holding up their cups until* ANDRA *drains her own. As she lowers her cup she is the first to see* SUE *enter from Left.* SUE *is in a pair of heavy flannel pajamas, with a trench coat pulled over them. She is gaunt and pale as she seems to float into the room. Her eyes seem to have lost all contact with the living. The* OTHERS, *turning to see what* ANDRA *has seen, stop singing.*]

SUE. [*In a strange distant voice.*] You're all having a party, aren't you—what a nice party—may I join you?

SMITTY. [*As to a child.*] Of course, Sue, but only for a minute. Remember, you promised to take a nice nap—

SUE. [*Seeing* ANDRA *for the first time.*] Why, Andra, whatever have you been doing? [*Brushes some dust off* ANDRA.] You'd better run up to your room and change.

ANDRA. Susan, you— [*She drops to her chair unable to finish.*]

SUE. You all must come to a party of mine some time—

NYDIA. [*With sincere understanding.*] We'd all love to, honey, it's sweet of you to ask us.

SUE. [*Suddenly she looks around the room startled.*] One—two—three—four—five—six—seven— Where are the rest? [*Eight happens to be* CONNIE, *whom she sees for the first time apart from the others. She stops and her tense attitude changes to one of solicitude as she walks over to* CONNIE'S *bunk.* CONNIE *puts down her book.*] Why weren't you at the party—weren't you invited?

CONNIE. [*Quietly.*] I didn't feel well enough, Sue—I've been a little tired.

SUE. [*Wisely.*] Tired—tired, I know—all the others must have been tired, too—there should have been sixteen, you know.

SMITTY. They couldn't come, Sue.

SUE. They'll come to my party. [*To* CONNIE.] You'll come, too, won't you?

CONNIE. I'd love to.

SUE. [*To* ANDRA, *although her eyes are focussed on space.*] We'll dress, of course. I'll tell the others, the ones who aren't here—they visit me when I'm alone in my little room. [*A look of horror comes into her eyes. She starts to whimper, then screams and covers her face.*]

ANDRA. [*Taking her arm.*] Come on, Sue—you must get back to bed.

SUE. [*To* ANDRA.] Yes, my bed—it's very little, too—[*They start off Left.*]—too little—that's strange—everything's growing little, isn't it? The whole world, and my room— [*Turning again to* ANDRA *as they near the door.*] I used to have a large room—remember?

[*They exit,* ANDRA *comforting her in a low voice. After they disappear there is a short silence broken only by the distant rumble of GUNS.*]

PAT. [*Suddenly.*] If they don't send her back soon, I'll be getting that way myself.

NYDIA. Poor thing, she's so sweet.

SMITTY. Cut it out, all of you. We've got plenty of reasons to be thankful.

PAT. Name six.

GRACE. I thought you were the one who was telling me about landing reinforcements.

[*PHONE rings.* SMITTY *makes no move for it. She is watching* PAT *intently.*]

NYDIA. [*The* GIRLS *all look at* PAT.] Reinforcements—

GRACE. Sure. Pat told me a little while ago they'll be landing some any night.

SMITTY. [*Takes this in and is about to speak as the PHONE rings again. She picks it up. Into phone.*] 63rd Auxiliary—Smith—

NYDIA. Honest?

FLO. [*To* PAT.] Is it true?

[PAT *is giving* GRACE *a dirty look, but she nods in answer to* FLO'S *question.*]

SMITTY. [*On phone.*] No, sir, she hasn't come in yet, have you tried R95? Yes, sir.

HELEN. So that's what you were askin' about?

PAT. [*To* GRACE.] Why don't you broadcast it?

GRACE. Why didn't you tell me it was a secret?

HELEN. [*To* PAT.] You sure listen in for your share of official business.

PAT. I wasn't listening in—someone happened to tell me.

SMITTY. [*On phone.*] She should be here any minute then—I'll have her call you— Yes, sir. [*Hangs up.*]

NYDIA. I hope you're right, Pat. My boy friend might be

with them. [*Her face drops, and she pouts.* SMITTY *catches* PAT'S *eye.* PAT *turns away.*] The meany-pie—he might at least have written me he was coming.

SMITTY. [*Crossing to* PAT.] Where did you hear about this landing, Pat?

PAT. [*In mock secrecy.*] Walter Winchell.

SMITTY. Stop clowning. It's hardly a thing to joke about.

PAT. What do you expect me to do, blab?

SMITTY. Call it that if you choose. I want to know where you heard that we're expecting reinforcements?

PAT. Find out for yourself.

[*The other* GIRLS *have been eating, trying not to pay any attention to the conversation. The door Center now opens and* DOC *enters.* SMITTY *is greatly relieved as she turns away from* PAT.]

DOC. [*As she enters.*] Hello, girls. [*She drops her gear on the desk.*]

SMITTY. The Colonel's been trying to reach you.

DOC. [*As she reaches for the field phone.*] No message? [SMITTY *shakes her head.*] Give me R57—Marsh calling—

SMITTY. [*As she starts out down Left.*] Can you come inside a minute after you're through?

DOC. Yes. [*Into phone.*] Speaking. That's right—he can reach me here when he's free. [*To the* GIRLS *as she hangs up.*] Well, girls, unless the Colonel has other ideas, you'll all get a good rest now. Smitty can send one of you to Observation. The rest of you can turn in. [*She exits Left.*]

FLO. Them's good news to this tired old body.

GRACE. Isn't that my luck? The first time I have a legitimate excuse to get some rest—I've got to share it with everybody. [STEVE *enters from up Right. They face each other briefly.* STEVE *breaks away and* GRACE *crosses to* PAT.] Sorry, kid—didn't mean to put you on the spot.

PAT. Aw—she's been lookin' for a chance to slap me down since we got here—now maybe she's happy.

HELEN. Why didn't you tell her where you heard it? Stupid.

PAT. They can fry me before I eight-ball some guy into losing his stripes.

FLO. [*Indicates* NYDIA *who has started knitting frantically.*] Well, you made somebody happy.

PAT. You notice she didn't waste much time passin' it on to the Doc.

HELEN. Quit grousing, she's probably showing the Doc to Adam.

[*The* DOC *enters from Left with* SMITTY.]

DOC. Girls—there is something rather important I think you all should hear. [*The* GIRLS *wait silently for the* DOC *to continue.* PAT, *ignoring her, slowly starts out Right.*] Conlin, Conlin!

PAT. [*Stops and throws a venomous look at* SMITTY.] Yeah?

DOC. There are several questions I'd like to ask you. [PAT *doesn't speak.*] On three occasions you've been reported away from duty—Tuesday night you left your post at

Observation and were gone almost an hour—is that correct?

PAT. [*Resenting this very much.*] I suppose so.

DOC. Yesterday afternoon, just before the heavy barrage started, you were gone for about the same time.

PAT. [*Shortly.*] That's right.

DOC. And you were absent this afternoon? [PAT *doesn't answer.*] Well.

PAT. Sure, that's right, so what does it make me? Everybody knows we all take a blow every so often when things are quiet.

[STEVE *and* FLO *slowly move closer to* DOC *and* PAT. *The other* GIRLS *are tense.*]

DOC. We have every reason to believe you weren't alone during those periods.

PAT. It's not very hard for a girl to find company around here.

DOC. Were you with one of the girls?

PAT. That'd be a swell way to break the monotony.

DOC. [*Severely.*] I'd advise you to change your tone.

PAT. [*Angrily.*] If you don't know who I was with, don't expect me to tell you. Where is all this supposed to be leading anyway? If I've broken any more of your stupid rules, tell me what's coming to me and let's get it over with.

DOC. I'm afraid it's a little more serious than that. Information has been passed on to the enemy steadily since you arrived here. We've been watching you and strangely enough your little absences from duty coincide with the enemy's successful attacks on each strong position.

PAT. [*Fear in her eyes for the first time as she realizes the seriousness of the accusation.*] It's a damned, rotten lie— [*She starts at* SMITTY, *but* FLO *and* STEVE *restrain her.*] This is your dirty work. You've had it in for me since we got here and you've tried to get me, but you can't get away with it.

DOC. [*Raising her voice.*] You can drop that talk. If Smitty had given me this information when she discovered it, this whole sector might be a lot stronger than it is today.

PAT. [*Frantically, starting to struggle.*] It's a lie—you can't pin a thing on me—

DOC. [*Interrupting again.*] I'll admit you've been very clever, but unless you can tell us who you've been working with, you'll be held here for court-martial.

CONNIE. Pat, tell them.

PAT. I'm not telling anything.

DOC. [*To* FLO.] Lock her in the store room.

[FLO *and* STEVE *start half-carrying her out Left.*]

PAT. [*To* SMITTY.] Wait till I get out of this, I'll stuff every filthy lie you've told about me right back where it came from. I'll settle with you, you lousy blab-bag. Wait till I get out of here I'll kill that dame—

[*She is pulled out struggling. The* GIRLS *watch in silence. The PHONE rings and* DOC *answers it.*]

DOC. [*At phone.*] 63rd Auxiliary—Marsh— Yes, Colonel— Yes, I understand— Yes sir—I know—as quickly as possible. [*She turns from the phone and looks at the silent ring of faces.*] All you volunteers are leaving immediately. Get your gear and personal things together and report to the supply depot. [*Starting for door Right.*] Your trucks are being loaded now, so you haven't much time. [*To* SMITTY.] Smitty.

[DOC *and* SMITTY *exit Right. All of the* GIRLS *but* ANDRA *move obediently to their bunks and start to get their gear together.*]

ANDRA. Wonder where they're sending us?

HELEN. I don't care as long as we get out of here.

ANDRA. [*Crossing to the door down Left.*] Steve—come on—[STEVE *enters; crosses to her bunk.*]—hurry and get your stuff together, we're leaving.

STEVE. Leaving?

ANDRA. Yes, hurry.

FLO. [*Standing in door down Left.*] What's happened?

ANDRA. That's what we'd like to know—they're moving all of us somewhere.

FLO. Where?

CONNIE. What do we care—even Cab Cabin was better than this filthy place.

GRACE. This war's turning out to be a junket of one-night stands.

SMITTY. [*Entering from up Right.*] Move fast—those trucks won't wait.

CONNIE. [*Ready with her bag.*] Where are they sending us?

SMITTY. You're being evacuated to another sector with as many of the wounded as the trucks can carry.

HELEN. I hope it's one the Japs never heard of—

ANDRA. You mean we're being evacuated just when it's getting to the point when we're really needed.

SMITTY. The Japs have started to move which may be a trick or a big drive for Bataan—if it continues, this whole sector could be cut off.

ANDRA. But I don't understand—

SMITTY. There's nothing to understand—you've heard your orders.

ANDRA. What about Sue?

SMITTY. You'll take her with you.

NYDIA. [*Crossing down Center.*] Well, I'm ready, but I just know I've forgotten something.

SMITTY. [*To the* GIRLS.] Hurry up— [*To* ANDRA.] I'll get Sue and give her something to quiet her. [*Exits down Left.*]

[*GUNS are heard in the distance.*]

FLO. [*Seeing* GRACE *needs help.*] Grace, I'll help you. Do me a favor, will you?

GRACE. [*As she is crossing up Center.*] Name it.

FLO. Mail a letter for me—if you happen to pass a box. [*Following her up stage.*]

GRACE. Sure, but you'd better write fast—

FLO. This one's been written for a long time.

NYDIA. That reminds me—where are all those letters we've been writin' for the boys?

ANDRA. [*Crossing down Left to cabinet.*] Here, I'll get them—

HELEN. Gee, if what Smitty says is true—these might be the last letters to go out of here.

[ANDRA *has passed letters to* FLO *who has added hers and given packet to* GRACE.]

[*WARN CURTAIN*]

GRACE. [*Taking letters.*] Damn it—I'd like to know who's goin' to take care of all these guys? Who's goin' to take our place here?

STEVE. They could send more back if we didn't go, couldn't they—

[*The GUNS are heard again.*]

CONNIE. Stop it—do you all want to stay here and end up like Sue?

ANDRA. We couldn't take Sue out through that barrage —she'll have to stay. I'm going to stay with her.

GRACE. Me too. A trip out of here in one of those trucks, with this leg would kill me. Helen, here take these. [*Hands her the letters.*]

HELEN. [*Taking the packet from* GRACE. *She is all silent for a moment, looks at the letters then at* ANDRA. *Then suddenly turns to* NYDIA—*handing her the letters.*] I just remembered somethin' I promised a guy I'd do— [*Running off Right.*]

NYDIA. [*Looking after* HELEN *for a moment, puzzled.*] What's she cryin' about?

SMITTY. [*Entering from down Left and taking in the situation.*] What's the matter with all of you?

GRACE. It's no use, Smitty—there may be one or two of us who haven't quite decided how much our penny ante help means to these guys up here. [DOC *enters. The* GIRLS *do not see her.*] We don't want to put you on a spot, but we're in this war as much as you and Flo—maybe we're not nurses, but you know damned well you need us.

SMITTY. You haven't the right to—

GRACE. Just a minute, Smitty—if guys like you can't decide by now when we have a fight then we'd better turn in our suits and learn to goose step—we might not be much help but if we're not allowed to try then someone else is wrong—not us.

STEVE. What will they do to us if we stay?

DOC. [*Moving into the group.*] Be very proud to have you here— Word has just come through— [*The* GIRLS *turn.*] The Japs have broken up our relief convoy from Cebu— Evacuation now is, of course, impossible.

CURTAIN

ACT THREE

SCENE I

It is shortly before dawn the following morning. HELEN, GRACE, FLO, NYDIA *and* ANDRA *are in their bunks.* STEVE *is at door, up Center, which she holds slightly open and looks out into the night. In the distance is heard the continuous rumble of GUNS. Slowly she closes the door and starts down the steps.* GRACE *rises on her elbow.*]

GRACE. [*Calling quietly.*] Steve—Steve—

[STEVE *ignores her.*]

FLO. [*Raising her head.*] Steve— [STEVE *stops and looks up at her.*] Anythin' new?

STEVE. Mr. Moto's kept the barrage goin' all night.

GRACE. [*Trying to get into the conversation.*] I heard every shell. [STEVE *continues to ignore her and lowers herself into* PAT'S *bunk.*] Hey, Flo—come here.

FLO. [*Sits up and stretches, gets down slowly, crosses to* GRACE.] Get any sleep?

GRACE. No—even if I felt like it, this leg wouldn't let me.

FLO. Want me to change the dressing?

GRACE. No, thanks—wish you could change the leg.

FLO. The guns been going all night, eh?

GRACE. Never missed a beat. Had a lot of competition around here, though.

FLO. What's happened?

GRACE. [*Forcing lightness.*] Andra's been bringing down Zeros from her bunk all night, and Helen's dreamed her way through half the Army.

FLO. How about me?

GRACE. [*Disgustedly.*] You snore.

FLO. [*After a pause, more seriously.*] I couldn't get Pat off my mind.

GRACE. Me, too.

FLO. Kinda hard to swallow, wasn't it?

GRACE. If we ever get through this, I won't trust my own mother.

FLO. [*Quickly.*] Don't say that.

GRACE. What?

FLO. I know what you meant— Sorry.

GRACE. Don't be. [*Regretfully.*] I did hurt her badly once—

FLO. I think we all must, in different ways.

GRACE. She thought I'd lied to her—I hadn't really—

FLO. She understood.

GRACE. Perhaps—I wish I were sure.

HELEN. [*Rolling over.*] Why don't you guys let a fella get a little rest?

GRACE. [*Changing quickly.*] Was that what you were having?

HELEN. First peace I've had in a week.

GRACE. Was it good?

[FLO *has moved to the table.*]

NYDIA. [*Sits up.*] Goodness gracious, is it time to get up already?

FLO. [*Looking at watch.*] Four-twenty.

NYDIA. [*Petulantly.*] Four-twenty? Then why don't you all go back to sleep?

HELEN. Every so often you really do get an idea, don't you? [*She rolls over and pulls the blankets over her head.*]

GRACE. You've got something to go back to.

NYDIA. [*Moving toward Left.*] Oh, gosh!

FLO. What's the matter?

NYDIA. Is there anything the matter?

FLO. With you?

NYDIA. Me? Oh nothing's the matter—I just found out I've gotta go.

GRACE. Psychic, eh?

NYDIA. No, I didn't. [*Exits Left.*]

ANDRA. [*Turning over.*] What's up?

FLO. Only Nydia.

ANDRA. What a good rest—I've the appetite of a cannibal. [*Jumps out of bed.*]

HELEN. [*Brought upright by the sound.*] Looks like I'd better give up.

ANDRA. Anyone care for a sandwich?

HELEN. I suppose I could use one.

ANDRA. Anyone else? [*She stands in the Left doorway.*]

[*They shake their heads.*]

FLO. Not for me—[ANDRA *turns.*]—Take it easy when you pass that baby.

ANDRA. I'm not that hungry—really. [*Exits Left.*]

GRACE. Sadie'll see that nobody disturbs that kid.

FLO. She's certainly taken with him.

GRACE. She's sore because she can't nurse him.

HELEN. How is she going to feed him?

FLO. Haven't you seen the bottle she's rigged up?

GRACE. No.

FLO. An old ether bottle—she's tied a rubber glove onto it and put a hole in one of the fingers.

HELEN. Yeah?—but what does she put in the bottle?

GRACE. Canned milk—I suppose. [HELEN *gags.*] Nothin's better.

[NYDIA *returns, hiking her girdle.*]

FLO. Feelin' better?

[HELEN *gets down from bunk.*]

NYDIA. Oh, sure—say, Pat's making an awful fuss in that store room.

HELEN. She'd be doing a lot worse than that if I could get my hands on her.

GRACE. I thought we'd decided not to talk about that?

FLO. She doesn't mean it.

HELEN. [*Angrily.*] The hell I don't. The way she sold us out, I'd like to hold that court-martial right here.

FLO. [*Evenly.*] Grace's right—we all agreed not to talk about that.

DOC. [*Enters from Right and takes up the field phone. It seems out of order and she jiggles the hook several times. She then turns to the* GIRLS.] Steve.

FLO. [*Quickly.*] She's asleep, I think.

DOC. Don't disturb her. Flo, you'd better—

STEVE. [*Sleepily, rising.*] Did you call me, Doc?

DOC. You were asking for some air—still want to go?

STEVE. Yes, I'd like to.

DOC. The field phone seems to be out of order. Trace the line back to Observation, and if you can find the break, report it. [STEVE *takes her helmet and kit from her bunk.*] On your way back, stop by the depot and see if we left any quinine there yesterday.

STEVE. Sure, Doc. [*Exits Center and* DOC *starts out Right.*]

FLO. [*To* DOC.] Need any help in there?

DOC. Not immediately, thanks. [*Exits Right.*]

GRACE. Poor Steve, I wouldn't want to check that line out there alone.

HELEN. Yeah, maybe I'm wrong, but it seems a lot thicker than it was yesterday.

GRACE. I wonder why those Jap-pansies keep pounding us. There's not much left here to shoot at.

HELEN. Maybe they're our reinforcements.

FLO. You'll hear a bigger noise than that when they arrive. [ANDRA *enters Left with a tray of food and more tea.* FLO *reaches for one of the sandwiches.*] I think I'll change my mind—

ANDRA. Change it in the kitchen—these are spoken for.

[ANDRA *slaps her hand and* FLO *shrugs and starts Left for kitchen.*]

GRACE. [*Calling after* FLO.] Get one for me, Flo.

ANDRA. [*Taking one to* GRACE.] I figured you'd change your mind.

HELEN. [*Biting into a sandwich.*] Gee, this hits the spot.

[*The door Center opens and* CONNIE *enters looking worn, dirty and dog tired. She is more nervous than we have seen her before. Her nerves seem about to give out. She crosses to get her soap and private towel.*]

GRACE. Well, if it isn't our little baby-face, and does your hair need setting.

NYDIA. I hope you don't feel as bad as you look, honey.

HELEN. One of the boys try to persuade you—

CONNIE. [*Turning on them.*] How can you sit there and joke when every word may be your last.

HELEN. Take off the shroud, will you. It's enough to know things are bad without draping it all over the walls.

ANDRA. [*Crossing to her at basin.*] You've got the wrong angle, Connie—I know. I felt the way you do until I discovered the mental beating that you can give yourself out here will tear you to pieces faster than any of those shells.

[CONNIE *starts back for her bunk.* FLO *gives* ANDRA *the eye.*]

CONNIE. Leave me alone—can't you?

NYDIA. I'm awfully sorry, honey, if anything I said—

CONNIE. I'm afraid I'm different from the rest of you—

HELEN. [*As* CONNIE *goes toward her bunk.*] Cut it out —who relieved you at Observation?

CONNIE. [*Putting on perfume.*] Smitty.

ANDRA *and* GRACE. Smitty!

CONNIE. Yes, she said you were asleep.

HELEN. Was Lieutenant Holt there?

CONNIE. He came up with her.

[*They* ALL *exchange knowing looks.*]

HELEN. I'd like to see him trying to open that icebox.

GRACE. Jealous, dear?

HELEN. I've been able to handle him, which is doing more than some others I could mention.

GRACE. He's never alone, is he? I'll bet the shell that finds him will get two for one.

NYDIA. Why, I think you're all perfectly nasty about Lieutenant Holt. Why, he's the—

GRACE. [*Interrupting as* FLO *enters.*] —smoothest—

HELEN. —the cagiest—

FLO. —wolf—that ever wore a uniform.

[NYDIA *has looked from one to the other as they spill this out in perfect rhythm.*]

NYDIA. Well, he's always been perfectly nice to me.

HELEN. Maybe you've got something he doesn't want.

[*There is a sudden convulsion of the room. It is the heaviest SHOCK we have had yet. The lamp swings wildly. There is silence as the* GIRLS *watch it. Almost immediately another and more severe SHOCK rocks the room. In silence the cry of the baby is heard.*]

NYDIA. The lamp never shook that much before.

GRACE. It almost had our names on it.

HELEN. The ones to worry about are labeled "to whom it may concern."

[*There is another and bigger SHOCK. The lamp goes completely out and we see that the* GIRLS *are all knocked off their feet as the lamp flickers out. There are several muffled screams from off Right.*]

ANDRA. Get that lamp on.

NYDIA. Let's get out of here.

FLO. Don't open that door.

CONNIE. Light that lamp. Light it.

[*There is a general ad lib. A match flickers and we see* FLO *on a chair relighting the lamp. The explosion has tossed furniture over the floor, and the* GIRLS *are scat-*

tered, at the moment they are pulling themselves together. The cry of the baby is heard. FLO *is the first to see the dirt and dust coming from the passageway Right. She jumps from the chair and dashes into the passage.*]

FLO. The passage's caved in.

GRACE. The Doc's in there.

ANDRA. [*To* HELEN *as she starts after* FLO.] Come on—

[*They exit as* SMITTY *dashes in from Center.*]

NYDIA. It was the passage—the Doc's in there.

FLO. Under God knows how many tons of earth.

ANDRA. You couldn't get through there with a rotary plow.

SMITTY. [*Jumps into the passageway and almost immediately returns and starts out Center.*] Maybe we can get in through the other door— [*She exits.*]

NYDIA. [NYDIA'S *whimpers have broken into sobs. Suddenly she makes a burst for the passage.*] Doc—Doc Marsh— [FLO *grabs* NYDIA.] They can't kill her—she's still alive, I know it.

FLO. There isn't a chance. If there was any chance of getting to her, do you think we'd be standing here now?

NYDIA. [*Between screams and tears.*] Sure you would —you're afraid for your own lives—but I'm not—I'll get to her— [*She breaks from* FLO *and makes a dash.* ANDRA *steps in front of her.*] Let me go— She's still alive, I tell you. [NYDIA *breaks past* ANDRA, *crying for the* DOC. *Her cries turn into hysteria which come to us from the passageway.*] Doc—Doc Marsh—Doc Marsh — [*She re-enters wracked with hysteria.*]

ANDRA. [*Steels herself as* NYDIA *passes her.*] Shut up. [NYDIA *continues. With a quick movement,* ANDRA *swings her around and slaps her across the face.*] Shut up, I say. [NYDIA *resorts to dry sobs.*] Now stop making a blithering fool of yourself—any more of that screaming and I'll silence you until you get better sense.

HELEN. Stop talking that way.

ANDRA. [*In deadly earnest.*] I mean every word of it—we're all on a limb and I wouldn't think twice of removing any dead weight that might bring us down. Things are happening fast out there—it might never come, and it might come any minute—there's little we can do, but be ready for it.

FLO. [*Not seeing* SMITTY, *who has slowly entered from Center, shaken terribly by the loss of* DOC.] Come to think about it—things have been about like that ever since we've been up here, haven't they?

SMITTY. Thanks, Flo, we've all got to look at it that way. That's the way she always looked at it and I'm sorry she isn't here now to see the end of the sneaking bitch responsible for all this.

HELEN. [*Starting for the door Left.*] Let's get her out here now, and—

SMITTY. [*Quickly interrupting.*] Wait a minute—we were all wrong about Pat. I've been doing a little checking and discovered where she was during those absences. Pat was with an officer and he's cleared her completely, but there's one girl whose actions look damned suspicious and I want an explanation right now!

[*The* GIRLS *watch* SMITTY *expectantly as she turns toward the bunks Right. At that moment,* CONNIE *slips out of her bunk. She holds a small revolver in her hand which she holds pointed at* SMITTY'S *belt.*]

CONNIE [*Her voice is hard and cold.*] Stand where you are all of you. [*Then, almost tauntingly to* SMITTY.] Too bad you didn't shoot me when you had the chance.

SMITTY. Our laws provide trials, even for rats like you.

CONNIE. A mistake—we are taught to shoot first—justify it later. [ANDRA *makes a move.* CONNIE *swings the gun on her.*] Perhaps you don't believe me. [ANDRA *stops.*] Go on—get over there— [*Indicates side where* SMITTY *and the* OTHERS *stand, then to* GRACE *and* NYDIA.] You too— [*They cross. She is interrupted by the door Center swinging open as* STEVE *appears. She backs slowly down stage and keeps the* OTHERS *covered.* STEVE *looks at her, surprised, then at the* OTHERS.] Put up your hands —the rest of you stay where you are! [*With deep scorn.*] I've waited a long time for this—they said it would be easy but I never believed anything could be this easy.

STEVE. [*Moving toward* CONNIE.] Put it down, Connie —everything's going to be all right.

SMITTY. [*Realizing what might happen.*] Do what she says, Steve.

STEVE. Leave her alone—she wouldn't hurt any of you—

CONNIE. Stay where you are and put your hands up.

STEVE. No one's going to hurt you any more, Connie, you or me—

SMITTY. Steve!

CONNIE. [*Sharply.*] I'm not going to warn you again.

STEVE. [*Close to her.*] Please put it down—they just don't understand—

CONNIE. Another step and I'll blow you all over this floor—

STEVE. [*Stops for a moment, then smiles and as she steps forward.*] Not your old pal, Steve—

[CONNIE *fires three bullets into* STEVE'S *stomach.* STEVE *lurches forward, her face a mask of horrified bewilderment, as she slumps to the floor.* CONNIE *moves past her toward the Center door as the* OTHERS *are about to close in on her.*]

CONNIE. Stand back—there's your thanks for not shooting me, you yellow herd of polyglot sheep. [*Almost simultaneously there is a SHOCK which forces the door closed and throws all of the* GIRLS *to their knees.* CONNIE *quickly recovers and swings the gun on them. She tries to open the door with her left hand as she covers the room with the gun. It doesn't budge. The look of a caged animal crosses her face as she moves away a few steps.*] Come on, Girl Scouts—you've done everything else for me—now you can move that door— [*No one moves.*] Open it.

[NYDIA *moves slowly to the door.* HELEN *joins her and between them they try to open it. Even under their joint strength it refuses to budge.*]

SMITTY. [*Coolly as she lowers her hands.*] That was one thing you didn't figure on.

CONNIE. [*Somewhat shaken but still in full control.*] Keep—those—hands—up.

SMITTY. [*Easily, as she ignores the order.*] You've got

three bullets left in that gun, and I'm sure you've better sense than to think you can pull that trigger fast enough to get us all before we get you.

CONNIE. [*Casting glances Right and Left as she makes up her mind what she should do next.*] Three bullets and the first one's for you, Smitty.

[*The* GIRLS *have pulled themselves together somewhat because of* SMITTY. ANDRA *first, and then* GRACE *lower their arms.* NYDIA *and* HELEN *are the last to relax.*]

SMITTY. While you're trying to remember what your great Dictator told you to do in a case like this, I'm going to move Steve—[*She steps forward.*]—and probably give you the only chance you'll have to shoot one of us in the back. [SMITTY *moves up to* STEVE'S *body without looking at* CONNIE. *Deliberately she turns her back on the gun.*]

[*The other* GIRLS *watch* CONNIE *for a sign of action but she seems to be sifting every possibility hastily in her mind.* ANDRA *steps forward.*]

CONNIE. [*Quickly covering her.*] No, you don't—Smitty can handle it.

[*WARN CURTAIN*]

ANDRA. Be a good sport and try stopping me.

[FLO *joins* ANDRA *and* SMITTY *who are putting* STEVE *on* GRACE'S *bunk.*]

NYDIA. [*Completely frustrated.*] You—you contemptible —I wish there was something I could do.

CONNIE. [*Shoving her and* HELEN *from the door.*] Shut up.

NYDIA. I'll do nothing of the sort.

HELEN. Shut up, Nydia.

[NYDIA *looks at her and subsides.* SMITTY *and* ANDRA *whisper.* ANDRA *is speaking so quietly that even* CONNIE *can't hear her.* SMITTY *shakes her head.*]

CONNIE. Stop that whispering.

SMITTY. [*Crossing toward* CONNIE.] Your training in German methods has been very thorough.

CONNIE. It should be— I was trained in one of the best Bunds in your country.

ANDRA. [*Starting for* CONNIE.] This is ridiculous, I'd like to have a look at that blood she's been braggin' about.

SMITTY. [*Stopping her.*] Do you want to take the responsibility for any more deaths?

ANDRA. [*Angrily.*] I don't intend to stand around and do nothing.

SMITTY. She's cornered and she knows it, but she's got enough sense not to start something she knows she can't finish. Until someone loses her head, no one will be hurt. [*Starts slowly toward* CONNIE.] We might be here for a long time—we can sleep and eat and she can't. [*Stops at table and turns to* OTHERS.] Now relax, all of you. We'll let her make the mistake. We'll be ready for it.

[SMITTY *sits. All of the* GIRLS *slowly ease themselves into chairs and* ANDRA *lights a cigarette as the Curtain slowly falls.*]

CURTAIN

ACT THREE

SCENE II

SCENE: *Several hours have passed since the end of the preceding Scene. The tension in the room has increased to the breaking point. The* GIRLS, *other than* CONNIE, *are doing an excellent job of trying to be casual.* FLO *whistles softly as she reads one of her old letters from "Mom."* ANDRA *and* GRACE *are playing rummy at the table and* NYDIA *is busy "kibitzing" and knitting.* SMITTY *sits on the edge of one of the bunks, busy making pencil entries in her record book.* HELEN *sleeps fitfully on the bunk nearest the table.* CONNIE, *at the moment, is trying to light a cigarette without taking her eyes from the* OTHERS *in the room.* GRACE *or* ANDRA'S *sudden movement with a card is making this difficult.*

NYDIA. That messy old lamp seems to be runnin' out of something again.

FLO. I filled it this morning.

ANDRA. The wick seems to be all right.

GRACE. Maybe it's havin' as much trouble gettin' fresh air as we are—

NYDIA. [*To* FLO.] I wish you would whistle another tune. That one is so depressing.

GRACE. How about some knitting music, maestro?

ANDRA. I like it. Reminds me of that first day we came up here. She was right where she is now, whistling and reading one of those letters from home.

FLO. Same one.

GRACE. Less than a month ago—

ANDRA. Several lifetimes—

GRACE. [*Slaps her cards down.* CONNIE *loses another light.*] Gin! [*Looks at* SMITTY.] Writin' letters, Smitty?

SMITTY. Cleaning up a few odds and ends the Doc left.

FLO. Sorta closin' books.

SMITTY. Sorta—

GRACE. [*Tossing the cards to* ANDRA.] Hundred and seventy-three you owe me—had enough?

ANDRA. One more.

GRACE. Deal 'em up—Helen's sleepin' into overtime—somebody else's shift—Smitty—how about you breakin' down and catchin' forty winks. [*Pokes* HELEN *with crutch.*]

HELEN. [*Sitting up suddenly before* SMITTY *can answer.*] No—no— [*Looks round in fright.*] My God. I run into the damndest things when my eyes are closed.

GRACE. You ought to keep a night diary.

HELEN. [*Nodding at* CONNIE.] How's sugar plum been behaving?

GRACE. She's workin' up hot pants for the Jap Corporal who's gonna break through our lines an' dig her out.

HELEN. [*Jumping down.*] Peculiar taste in bedfellows, these Nazis.

NYDIA. Somebody ought to be missin' us along about now.

HELEN. Johnny?

GRACE. —Or Lieutenant Holt?

SMITTY. [*Sharply.*] One of you had better try to cork off for a while.

[GRACE *and* ANDRA *cut cards for the bunk.* GRACE *shrugs and slips into it. The GUNS start up nearby.*]

GRACE. I'll go through the motions but I won't promise results.

NYDIA. Oh, darn it—there go our guns again—it was quiet for so long I was hoping the war was over.

HELEN. What would you do if it was, Lambie-pie?

NYDIA. I'd go straight home and grow old gracefully.

[SADIE *enters Left with a tray of sandwiches and steaming coffee. She is obviously frightened of* CONNIE. *As she starts to put the tray on the table* CONNIE *points the gun at her.*]

CONNIE. Bring that over here. [SADIE *hesitates. In cold menacing voice.*] Bring it here or you'll get what I gave Steve.

[SADIE *starts to comply but* ANDRA *takes the tray.*]

ANDRA. Oh no, you don't.

SMITTY. [*Walks between* SADIE *and* CONNIE, *her back to* CONNIE.] How's Pat? [SADIE *can't speak from fright.*]

Did you tell her everything that's happened? [SADIE *nods.*] Go back and tell her we'll let her out as soon as we take care of a little matter in here.

SADIE. [*Backing toward the door.*] Yes—yes—

ANDRA. [*Stopping her.*] Is Sue all right?

SADIE. Yes—she's still sleeping—she and the baby—

[SMITTY *nods for her to exit and they resume their previous positions.* SMITTY *turns to* CONNIE.]

SMITTY. This is still America as far as we're concerned. If you want some food—help yourself.

ANDRA. Have you got a bone you could throw her?

[SMITTY *sits and picks up the record book.*]

GRACE. Say, what is your pay-off for this deal—what did you expect your sawed-off pals'd pin on you—the Jap double cross—

CONNIE. When they're through pinning things on you—you'll regret these stupid attempts to be clever.

HELEN. [*Holding out tray.*] Bologna?

CONNIE. What an inferior bunch of cattle you really are with your moving picture idea of heroics and stiff upper lip—right now while your musical comedy army is being pushed around—while all of your little toys are being taken from you—you bask in the conceit that everything must have a happy ending— How?—Did you ever stop to think how?

GRACE. What do you think's going on back in the States right now, dearie?

CONNIE. [*Viciously.*] Strikes—big shots keeping the

tools of war from being made because of money or politics— Labor union racketeers kidding the dumb laborers that now is the time to get even with those big shots—and so, more strikes. An inferior race that needs the regimentation of the German master race, and hasn't long to wait.

HELEN. No wonder you use such strong perfume.

FLO. Funny thing about your kind—you've never really understood our kind—and there's not so much to understand when you boil it down. Take what's left of us here—we're a pretty average bunch—we're not heroes—we're not even soldiers—we're just a bunch of scared girls who hate war and death almost as much as we hate what your superior race has to offer—"Superior race"—that's a beautiful way to describe a people who twist their men into cold machines and turn their women into breeding animals—into cows who are graded by the calves and milk they can produce. No—you keep your way, we'll take ours, but this time we'll make you understand us so completely that you'll never forget, because this time—we understand you. Give me a cigarette.

ANDRA. [*Giving her one.*] Didn't know you used them.

FLO. My first—suppose there's a lot of things I should have tried before this.

[*There is a short silence.* NYDIA *wipes her face with her sleeve. All of the* GIRLS *are sweating. The lamp seems to be growing dimmer.*]

PAT. [*Off Left.*] I'll show that Nazi rat— I'll pull her apart, the dirty little—

SMITTY. Pat!

GRACE. Sadie's let her out.

CONNIE. [*Pulling back on the bunk.*] Keep her out of here.

PAT. [*Off.*] Leggo me—

SMITTY. [*Starting for the door.*] That wild Irishman'll botch everything—

CONNIE. You stay here.

[*As* SMITTY *turns toward* CONNIE, PAT *dashes in.* SMITTY *grabs her and* FLO *also restrains the dirt-covered, wild-eyed* PAT.]

SMITTY. Cool off, Pat, she's got an automatic.

SMITTY. Keep your head.

PAT. [*Looking for* CONNIE *frantically.*] And save yours —is that it?

FLO. Sit down, Pat—

PAT. Where's that Nazi rat?

[*She sees* CONNIE *at last and tries to make a dash for* CONNIE, *who draws a bead on her.* SMITTY *slugs her and she slumps to the floor. They raise her and start to lift her on* ANDRA'S *bunk.*]

NYDIA. How is she?

FLO. Asleep, but it was her turn anyway.

SMITTY. She'll be trouble when she comes out of it.

HELEN. And it won't be long, she's got a good Irish head.

GRACE. [*To* CONNIE.] You can come out from under your rock now, dearie.

HELEN [*Crossing to door Center.*] Shhh.

[*They* ALL *look at her. She is listening at the door.*]

ANDRA. What is it?

HELEN. I'd swear I heard some men up there.

CONNIE. [*Menacing* HELEN *as she cautiously moves toward door.*] Get back from that door.

ANDRA. Imagination.

[HELEN *moves away from door.* CONNIE *takes her place listening.*]

GRACE. I don't know— Helen's usually got a good ear for men.

NYDIA. I thought I heard something too, but nobody said anything—

[PAT *groans and stirs.* FLO *moves beside her. So does* SMITTY.]

SMITTY. Sorry, kid.

PAT. [*With a slow look around, she sits up.*] What did you hit me with—Corregidor?

SMITTY. It had to be that way—

PAT. Pat, the mashuga, huh?

SMITTY. You did what we all would like to do—but a different way—

PAT. [*Getting back a little of her old fire.*] Sure, the easy way— I should of known.

GRACE. Cut it, Pat.

[FLO *is about to speak but* SMITTY *nods "no."*]

SMITTY. [*Moving toward door Center.*] Any time you feel like changing your mind, take a look at Steve.

ANDRA. [*To* PAT.] I suppose we owe you an apology for last night—

PAT. Forget it.

HELEN. Yes, we're all sorry, Pat, and—

NYDIA. Yes— I don't know what is the matter with me. [*Wipes her face.*] I—I feel terribly dizzy—it's a headache, I think—

HELEN. We've got to get some air in here.

FLO. [*Getting her some water.*] Take this.

[NYDIA *drinks it and perks up somewhat.* SMITTY *studies her and realizes it is just faintness. The air seems to be getting heavier.* HELEN *takes a glass of water and brings one to* GRACE. PAT *picks up a bottle which has slid out on the bunk.*]

PAT. [*Holding up bottle.*] Hey—what's this—look what I found—

SMITTY. [*Crossing to her.*] Give me that bottle.

PAT. [*Laughing vindictively.*] Benzedrine and codein—so the little tin goddess has feet of clay after all. Her steel constitution's been comin' out of a bottle all this time— So you been showin' us up around here for weeks—tryin' to make us think you were better than we were—all the time you been swallowin' these pills for your courage—what a phoney.

[*The* GIRLS *are silent, some ashamed or embarrassed at* PAT'S *outburst.*]

SMITTY. That was a rotten trick, Pat—and not very funny. [*She takes the bottle and turns away.*]

[*The* GIRLS *for the most part avert their eyes as* PAT *turns to them.*]

FLO. [*Quietly to* PAT.] You owe her an apology.

PAT. [*Annoyed.*] The hell I do.

FLO. [*Significantly.*] Yes, you do.

PAT. What do you mean?

FLO. The Doc made her take those when she had her stomach torn open and passed up a transfusion for one of the boys.

PAT. [*Flushing.*] On the level?

FLO. It's hardly the time for lies, is it?

PAT. I'm sorry— [*She turns to* SMITTY, *having a hard time swallowing her pride.*] Smitty— [SMITTY *turns, ready for anything.*] Mind comin' over here— I want the others to hear what I got to say. [SMITTY *comes down slowly.*] I'm beginnin' to see what there is about me you don't like— I'm kinda thick-headed that way—but in time it sinks through. [SMITTY *starts to speak.*] No— let me get this off my chest first. It just happens you're the first women I've ever been jealous of—yeah, jealous. Since we've been up here, you've always done the things I've wanted to do—the way I've wanted to do them. Everybody always looked up to you—where I come from everybody always looked up to me. [SMITTY *starts to speak again.*] I'm not quite through yet—there's the little matter of Lieutenant Holt. [SMITTY *stiffens.*] I wanted him. Sure I could have had him—but not the way I wanted him—all to myself. I wasn't around him much before I saw that was out—there was only one of us who could have him that way and that was you.

SMITTY. Cut it out, Pat.

PAT. There's not much else to say. Every way I'd turn, I'd run into you and until tonight, I've never had brains enough to admit you were the better man—[*Offers her hand.*]—will you shake on it? [*They shake.*] I've never done this before, but I gotta admit I feel a lot better now I got it off my chest.

GRACE. [*Coming forward with her hand out to* SMITTY.] Will you give me a little of the same while you're at it, Smitty? I wouldn't have said what I did if I'd—

SMITTY. [*Interrupting her.*] It's all right, Grace. It wasn't news to me, only I didn't want to hear it that way—

GRACE. [*A little timidly.*] You are kinda crazy for the guy, aren't you?

SMITTY. I was—when I married him.

[*The statement falls on the group like a bomb. They gasp.*]

FLO. [*Sympathetically.*] You still love him—

SMITTY. [*About to deny it, but she realizes it is all too evident.*] The hell I— [*Smiles at* FLO.] It's a hard habit to break.

NYDIA. Well, I think he's very nice man.

[*The* GIRLS *all laugh.* HELEN *seems to hear something at the Center door and goes to it.* ANDRA *follows. They* BOTH *listen.*]

GRACE. Just keep on thinking those nice things about everybody and you'll live to a nice ripe old age.

[HELEN *makes a sudden move for the door Center. There is the sound of DIGGING off. The other* GIRLS *converge on the door.* CONNIE *starts toward them.*]

HELEN. They're clearing the passage.

CONNIE. Get way from that door.

SUE. [*Who enters Left unnoticed.*] Why didn't you all come to my tea?

[ALL *turn toward* SUE *who is advancing toward* CONNIE.]

ANDRA. [*Starting toward* SUE.] Susan—

[SUE *is too near* CONNIE *before* ANDRA *can reach her.* CONNIE *is cornered by* SUE'S *approach.*]

SUE. [*To* CONNIE.] You promised you'd come, why didn't you come?

CONNIE. [*Her voice firm with effort.*] Go on back to your party—

SUE. [*Still approaching* CONNIE.] You had a special invitation, you know—and Steve did so want to see you—she came rather late, with the Doc.

CONNIE. [*Shaking noticeably.*] Get out of here, you *imbecile!* [*To* OTHERS.] Put her back in her cell.

[ANDRA *moves forward.*]

SUE. [*Somewhat startled by the outburst, she backs up, then seeming to notice the gun for the first time, she reaches for it.*] Why are you playing with that? [*Keeps walking to* CONNIE *until she is almost on top of her.*]

CONNIE. [*Hysterically.*] Get out of here, I tell you. Go on back to your ghosts. [*She throws* SUE *back into* ANDRA'S *arms.* SMITTY *goes to help* ANDRA *with* SUE.] Stand back. [*She covers the* GIRLS *and moves toward the Center door. She tries it—it moves.*] I've got one chance to get out of here and you are going to do as I say—

PAT. Like hell we are.

CONNIE. If you don't— I take Smitty first— Think that over. [*They hesitate.*] Now stand back and listen.

FLO. Talk fast.

CONNIE. I'm going out of here. The rest of you are going to stay—tell your boys there that you're packing—tell them anything—but give me ten minutes—after that, I don't care what you do—

PAT. Are you through?

CONNIE. It's that or Smitty's finish—and anybody else I can get. Now stand back—

[CONNIE *tries the door again—it opens. There is no one in the opening. Then, from above a voice in thick Jap accent, cries down.*]

JAP VOICE. Come up—Reeve guns berow.

[*At once they realize that the Japs have taken the sector.*]

NYDIA. Why, they're not our boys.

CONNIE. [*Laughing hysterically.*] So long—suckers. [*She turns and starts up the stairs hurriedly.*]

SMITTY. [*Shouting as she moves toward door.*] Look out, she's got a gun.

CONNIE. [*Trying to drop gun as she realizes the position she's in.*] No! [*There is a sharp report.* CONNIE *crumples and rolls down a few steps. She lies there.*]

JAP VOICE. Others come out with hands up—or we brow you out.

[*The* GIRLS *look at* SMITTY.]

SMITTY. [*To* GIRLS.] Grab what you want—and hurry. [*Calls out door.*] Give us a minute to get our clothes.

JAP VOICE. You get rater—come now—no tricks or you get burret like other girl—come.

SMITTY. All right.

GRACE. What'll we do?

SMITTY. [*Bracing herself.*] We have no choice. Get your kit together and let's go up before they decide to "brow" us out.

HELEN. [*Pathetically.*] Where is our army—our reinforcements— [*She sobs dry sobs and sinks on the bunk.*]

PAT. Stick it out, kid—all this means is a short vacation in a "con" camp till Ole Mac can get organized.

[HELEN *just shakes her head.*]

JAP VOICE. You come out or we brow you out—

SMITTY. Just a minute. [*To* GIRLS.] Hurry.

[*The* GIRLS *hurriedly break up and quickly pull little personal things from their bunks.*]

JAP VOICE. How many down there?

SMITTY. Nine. [*To* PAT *who stands beside her.*] Want to go first?

PAT. [*Appreciatively.*] Thanks, Skipper. [*She salutes* SMITTY *in a flip little way and starts up the stairs.*]

SMITTY. [*To* HELEN *who is grabbing her makeup.*] Come on, Helen, you won't need that stuff.

HELEN. There might be some men in the concentration camp. [*Knocks on wood as she speaks and starts up, continuing her makeup.*]

SMITTY. [*Crosses to* DOC'S *desk and piles papers into a wastebasket. She sets fire to them.*] Nydia—

NYDIA. [*Looking up from her search.*] I've lost my extra yarn—

SMITTY. [*Retrieving it.*] Here.

NYDIA. Thanks.

[*As* NYDIA *starts up the stairs,* ANDRA *leads* SUE *up the stairs.*]

ANDRA. Come, Susan—

SUE. Soon we'll all be together again, won't we? Won't Father and Mother be surprised—we'll have so much to tell them, won't we, Andra—won't we?

ANDRA. Yes, darling—yes—we'll have a lot to tell them—

[FLO *has been taking a long time at her bunk.* SADIE *enters Left with the baby.* GRACE *starts for the door on her crutches.*]

SADIE. How about the baby?

SMITTY. You go on up— I'll take care of him.

SADIE. [*Giving it up reluctantly.*] They won't hurt him, will they?

SMITTY. No, Sadie, he'll be all right. [SADIE *starts away with a parting look at the child.*] Give Grace a hand on the stairs, will you, Sadie?

[SADIE *turns and impulsively cuddles the baby and kisses him, then quickly goes to* GRACE *who is having a little trouble with the stairs.*]

[*WARN CURTAIN*]

GRACE. [*To* SADIE.] Thanks— [*Back to* SMITTY.] Do you know—this is the first time since I've come over here that I really haven't been afraid. [*You know she is frightened to death but she does a swell job of sticking out her chin.*]

[SADIE *helps her out of sight.* FLO *now comes out of the corner from her bunk.* SMITTY *is looking down at the baby.*]

FLO. [*Tucking a letter into her shirt.*] Well, Smitty—a swell ending, isn't it?

SMITTY. Maybe it's only the beginning—who knows?

FLO. [*She puts letter on the table.*] The folks at home'll be gettin' up about now—

SMITTY. I'll bet they're thinking of you.

FLO. Mom is— [*Opens her hand to show rabbit's foot.*] She gave me this rabbit's foot when I left—for luck—We ate the rabbit. [*Tosses foot up and catches it.*]

[*As she starts to toss it up again, there is the staccato sound of a machine GUN from above, punctuated by a shrill scream which is cut off in the middle.* FLO *and* SMITTY *stiffen where they stand.* SMITTY *slowly puts the baby on* ANDRA'S *bunk.* FLO *shudders and for a brief moment seems to be about to give out. Then she straightens and slowly looks at* SMITTY. *There are tears in her eyes.* SMITTY *straightens and returns* FLO'S *look—her face is set in hard lines, for a moment her head drops then her fists tighten. They look toward the door.* FLO *breaks the spell.*]

FLO. [*A slight tremor in her voice.*] Are you ready?

SMITTY. Are we ever?

[*They start out Center together, their steps steady. As they turn on the steps and start to disappear,* FLO *starts to whistle. They are out of sight when the machine GUN starts once more, cutting off the whistle. The GUNS stop. In the silence the Curtain starts down, a plaintive cry is heard from the baby.*]

THE CURTAIN FALLS

END OF THE PLAY

PROPERTY PLOT

On stage Act One

4 blankets
12 bottles in case
Matches—ash tray
Fly swatter
Magazines
Bundles of letters in desk
Pencil on table

Offstage Right

Small bottle for SMITTY
5 blankets; box of supplies; SMITTY's helmet and kit
Blood-stained stretcher
SMITTY's bag to set for Act Two
Bandage rolls to set for Act One, Scene II
CONNIE's gun set for Act Three
Soiled towel for SMITTY

Offstage Left

On tray—3 tin cups, 3 sandwiches on plate, tea pot, 2 sandwiches on plate
On tray—7 plates, 7 knives, forks and spoons, 7 cups, 6 slices of bread and butter
Coffee pot; pot of stew with spoon
Crutches; Baby; plate with 4 sandwiches; plate with 2 sandwiches
All suitcases; portable Victrola; duffle bag; letter and rabbit foot for FLO

5 packs of cigarettes and matches; basket and wooden bucket with pots and pans
9 Nurses' kits; 1 stretcher; blankets for SUE; wrist watches
DOC's bag; 4 fans; rolls of bandages in towel
2 large boxes full of medical supplies; splints; rolls of bandages; cheese cloth; many bottles of medicine; packages of salts, etc.
3 clip boards; medical charts; 1 field telephone; 9 pillows
9 army blankets; paper; pencils; 6 field notebooks various sizes
1 duffle bag for FLO
1 small bottle
Letter in envelope for FLO
12 suitcases—3 old, 2 very good looking and new; 1 duffle bag—6 others, various sizes
Packing for bags; dresses; slips; shoes; stockings; bath robes; make-up kits; combs; brushes; books, etc.
1 knitting bag with yarn; needles; back of sweater; toilet soap
Bottles of perfume for CONNIE
6 hand towels—8 bath
Cigarettes for PAT
12 large pots and pans; water bucket
3 tin cups; pill bottle (small), for SMITTY
Small bag with medical supplies for DOC
Deck of playing cards; tea pot large
6 cups and saucers; 12 tin plates; 12 knives, forks and spoons; bread and butter sandwiches; large kettle of stew
9 nurses' kits; rabbit's foot for FLO; 1 stretcher
1 blood-stained stretcher; 12 blood-stained towels
Smeared doctor's apron; pair of forceps; bottle of brandy for HELEN; pair of short crutches

3 trays
Practical automatic revolver for CONNIE
Baby wrapped in old blanket
Portable Victrola; bed pan; magazines
Playing cards; fly swatters; basket for NATIVE WOMAN

SOUND EFFECTS

ACT ONE

Scene I

Opening plane approaching and receding
Siren and planes
Explosion
Anti-aircraft guns
Distant explosion
All Clear (Siren)

Scene II

Explosion nearby
Siren
Explosions and dive bombers. Bombers continue until curtain.
Explosion more distant

ACT TWO

Anti-aircraft guns and planes
Baby cry
Explosion (Loud). Siren and explosion; distant bombs.
Anti-aircraft guns

ACT THREE

Scene I

At Rise—Distant guns and explosion
Explosion (Loud) Double with baby cry

Explosion (Extra loud)
Explosion (Loud)

Scene II

Anti-aircraft guns
Machine guns
Baby Cry

PROPERTIES TO BE CHOSEN BY DESIGNER

4 double deck hospital metal bunks. 6′ 4″ x 2′ 6″
1 medicine cabinet, regular army equipment. Type that is shipped in cartons and then set up. 2′ 0″ x 1′ 6″
1 box sink. Type that is used on ships. Look for in ship supply shop. 2′ 4″ x 1′ 6″
2 ammunition boxes, stenciled U. S. Army and type of ammunition; olive drab. 1′ 8″ x 2′ 8″ and 1′ 7″ high
1 earthen water jug on bamboo stand. 1′ 6″ overall, spout on bottom, etc.
1 box between two bunks S.R. 1′ 2″ square
1 bamboo table. 4′ 6″ x 2′ 3″
1 bamboo chair for table
1 bamboo stool for table
1 box used as stool, for table
Decorations for walls, snakeskins, palms, cocoanuts, etc.
2 candles to light up, set in bottles
1 acetylene lamp to light up and flicker, hanging Center.

PUBLICITY THROUGH YOUR LOCAL PAPERS

The press can be an immense help in giving publicity to your productions. In the belief that the best reviews from the New York and other large papers are always interesting to local audiences, and in order to assist you, we are printing below several excerpts from those reviews.

"It is vivid drama—is good theatre. Its all-women cast is an effective novelty. Last night's audience was certainly held to complete attention."

New York Daily News

"— an honest picture of valiant women who attended wounded Americans on Bataan."

New York Journal-American

"The situation is there and the people; now and then there is grainy humor and at the end there is sudden, bleak tragedy met with courage."

New York Sun

"The best thing about 'Cry Havoc' is the fact that it can hardly help reminding all of us back here that the so-called sacrifices we are making to win this war are puny indeed compared to what those in the front lines have gone through, and are going through, every day. Mr. Kenward's play was worth doing if only to help pound home that message."

New York Post

"—has taken its theme from one of the truly inspiring moments of the war."

New York Times

"—a timely and thrilling tribute to the nurses and women auxiliary volunteers who served through the hell of Bataan and Corregidor. I liked it far better than I liked 'The Eve of Saint Mark,' finding in it not only more positive values in bringing the realities of the war home to us than the Anderson play but also more of substance, not only better theatre but better drama. —This is a human tragedy that is terribly touching and real."

New York World-Telegram

"—fine, eloquent moments; simple, honest touches—"

New York Herald-Tribune

"Compelling, caustic revelation of human beings under fire.—Has much to recommend it to the thoughtful —a hard-hitting, down-to-earth piece of theatre which deals dramatically and realistically with that inescapable realism in the Pacific.—Biting, feminine humor and feminine tenderness."—

Chicago Herald-American

"It's a sound, solid, dramatic war-play, very much about this war we're fighting, and no doubt is left as to what we're fighting for.—Tells us movingly of America's spirit and America's bone-bred conviction that democracy is right—and of the American will to fight for it. You will find no windy heroics, no pauses in the fast, realistic action for declamatory monologues. The play shoots straight and hard, start to tragic finish.—The play has everything."

Chicago Sun

"Continuous and engrossing entertainment."

Chicago Daily Tribune

"Plenty of blood and thunder melodrama.—Play vivid with tense dialogue and comedy lines.—The results are excellent."

Chicago Times

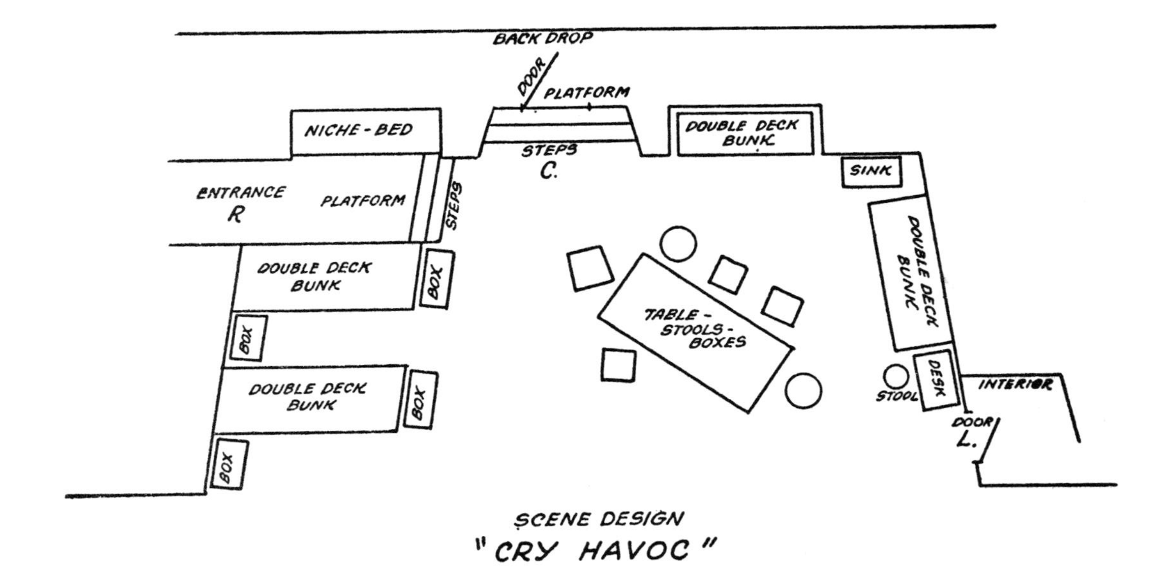

SCENE DESIGN
"CRY HAVOC"

Plays WITH A JEWISH THEME

ABIE'S IRISH ROSE

COLD WIND AND THE WARM, THE

COUNSELLOR AT LAW

DEAR ME, THE SKY IS FALLING

ENTER LAUGHING

FIFTH SEASON, THE

GOLEM, THE

HOLE IN THE HEAD

MAKE A MILLION

MAJORITY OF ONE, A

MIDDLE OF THE NIGHT

ONLY IN AMERICA

OUTRAGEOUS FORTUNE

POTASH AND PERLMUTTER

SEIDMAN AND SON

TENTH MAN, THE

UNCLE WILLIE

WALL, THE

WORM IN HORSERADISH, A

Going Ape

NICK HALL

(Little Theatre.) Farce.

3 male, 2 female—Interior

This hilarious and almost indescribable farce has some serious undertones. Rupert, an idealistic and romantic young orphan, has come to his uncle's house to commit suicide. This proves to be no easy matter. For one thing he is constantly attended by his uncle's attractive nurse/secretary. He is also constantly interrupted by a stream of visitors, at first fairly normal, but increasingly incredible. Rupert realizes that all the visitors are the same three people, and his attention is drawn toward understanding the preposterously Victorian plot in which he is trapped, and which, in a startlingly theatrical climax, he begins to understand. "An intricate plot with subtle foreshadowing and a grab bag of surprises . . . some of the funniest characters you'll ever see molded into a tight dramatic package."—News, Fort Myers. "Every scene transcends not only the imagination, but melds into a literally death-defying whole. It's fast, like 2,000 mph . . . a play as old and as contemporary as today." Sarasota Journal. "Going Ape is truly zany . . . the wackiness is infectious." —Time.

Eat Your Heart Out

NICK HALL

(Little Theatre.) Comedy.

3 male, 2 female—Interior

In this theatrical comedy Charlie, an out of work actor currently employed as a waiter, takes the audience through a sequence of hilarious encounters in a succession of Manhattan restaurants. By changing the tablecloths during the course of the action the basic setting of three tables and six chairs becomes a variety of New York restaurants, both elegant and shabby. The scenes change, the action is uninterrupted and the comedy never stops. The other performers play several parts: the girl desperately trying to eat snails and oysters to please her fiance; the middle-aged couple whose marriage is breaking up; the lovers so intent on each other they cannot order dinner; the rich, embittered astrologer; the timid man who never gets a waiter; the agents, directors, actors, and waiters. An amusing gallery of characters whose stories intertwine and finally involve Charlie. The author of "Accommodations" has written a very funny, contemporary play that is also a serious comedy of backstage life. ". . . a sharp, stunning play. It'll make you howl—but better yet, it might even make you sniffle a bit."—Fort Lauderdale News. "Tightly written and very, very entertaining. I recommend it enthusiastically."—Miami Herald. ". . . About as good as anything I've ever seen in dinner theater . . ."—Fort Lauderdale Times.

The Devil's Advocate

By DORE SCHARY

A Dramatization of the novel by Morris L. West

9 males, 2 females, extras—5 interiors

Leo Genn, Sam Levene, and Edward Mulhare headed the cast of this dazzling detection story about a dying priest who is sent, by his superiors, in the role of the devil's advocate to investigate and, if possible, discredit a dead man's claims to sanctity. The man was an Italian patriot who was beaten by the commies and finally killed by the nazis. Miracles are attributed to him. Was he a holy man, or a sinner? He was, it turns out, a bit of both. "The wonderful things which can be found in the theatre, in rare and golden moments—spirit, beauty, intelligence, skill, and the effect of transporting a playgoer far away from himself—came together with the production of 'The Devil's Advocate.' This is inspiring drama." —*N.Y. Daily News.*

Advise and Consent

By LORING MANDEL

Based on the Pulitzer Prize novel by ALLEN DRURY

DRAMA

18 males, 4 females, extras—CYC, WINGS, WAGON INSETS

Ed Begley, Richard Kiley, Henry Jones, Chester Morris, Staats Cotsworth, and Kevin McCarthy have some of the numerous juicy roles in this superb melodrama about the backstage politics in Washington during a subcommittee investigation of a man proposed for Secretary of State. Had the candidate been a communist? A witness says yes, but said witness begins to twitch and, under adroit cross-examination, comes apart at the seams. The crotchety old southern senator who produces the witness now appears to be only a sour-apple obstructionist. But is he? In the ensuing backstage intrigues one opportunistic senator so forces the issues that they end in calamity and in death for the subcommittee chairman. But on the floor of the senate the next day, the senior members restore the traditions of probity and honor.